The Cave of Branching Tales

The Cave of Branching Tales

and Other Fictions

Daniel W. Davison

THE
RAMSAY
PRESS

The Ramsay Press
3125 S Snoddy Road
Bloomington, Indiana 47401 USA

First Edition

Cover Art: Late 17th century print by Alain Manesson Mallet, photo-graphed from the author's private collection

Note on illustrations: The images in this book have been reproduced or modified from 19th and early 20th century publications that are now in the public domain.

ISBN: 0692380205
ISBN-13: 9780692380208

DEDICATION

For my brother Kyle Davison
21 January 1975–25 November 2014

Inquietum est cor nostrum,
donec requiescat in te.

CONTENTS

ACKNOWLEDGMENTS

I would like to thank both Dr. John Walbridge
of Indiana University and The Ramsay Press
for seeing this book through to publication.
I would especially like to thank my dear friend
and mentor, Ian Thomson, Professor Emeritus
of Classical Studies, for all of the encouragement and
sound criticism that he has given me through the years.

The Cave of Branching Tales

ROBED COURTIERS and eunuchs preceded and followed the muleteer and his son, who were driven more than escorted into the audience chamber. The two wore breeches and thong-strapped boots. Jade censers, waist-high, cast up thick clouds of incense so that the Son of Heaven's nose might not be offended by the stink of sweat and labor. The immobile presence on the throne, a youth in yellow brocade, looked beyond the visitors and into eternity.

The man and boy knelt, pressed their heads to the ground, and with their faces still to the carpet, looked at each other. The chief minister grinned and nodded, and with a flick of the hand encouraged the muleteer to proceed. The man rose and spoke in a rapid, clumsy manner with downcast eyes. "O Son of Heaven, we found a cave. It's under a mountain. My son can explain it. My son is clever and can read. I cannot."

The boy rose and looked directly at the Emperor, who was only slightly older than he: "The cave, Sir, is narrow at the mouth, but opens into a vast chamber dripping with stalactites and heavy with the pong of bat guano. In the middle of the cave, upraised on a smoothed dais, lies recumbent a bronze statue of Jum-Sum, god of sleep and dreams. His eyes are closed as if drowsing, but in his hand he holds a writing brush poised over a tablet on which he records the wonders men see in sleep. When we raised our torches over our heads, imagine our astonishment—"

"You would dare command the Emperor to imagine *your* astonishment?" said the chief minister, who had drawn himself up and was no longer smiling.

The boy lowered his eyes and sighed but did not kneel, although his father did. When he spoke again, he spoke quietly and in an unexpected manner, with a strange, cloying eloquence that surprised and at some remove intimidated everyone present: "We raised our torches and were astonished to see dark veins, maroon-hued, lining the entire wall—seemingly endless, running in parallel ribs, intersecting, irradiating, wound up in volutes.

They filled the surface of the rock, and continued into the shafts, sub-chambers, and cavities that dotted and honeycombed the cave. It was as if an army of ants—as if all the ants that had ever lived were marching off into battle. When we examined them closely, we noticed that these ribbons were actually brush-strokes forming characters, words and phrases.

"The first sentence I came upon, Son of Heaven, was the end of a story written in reverse with its beginning lost in an aperture high up in the ceiling. I traced it as far as I could. I stood a-tiptoe"—and here the boy rose up on his toes as he spoke. "I cannot remember much of it, but the closing sentence was 'And so ends the tale of the winged tigress of Penglai Mountain, who broods over her eggs for 10,000 years.'

"There was another story, which was actually two stories—two lines of text converging on the word *love*. One thread read 'And that is how the Duke of Chou lost his heart and came to despise *love*.' While the other read, 'And that is how the archer Shang-Li found *love*.' From that point on the fused sentence continued with a digression into yet another story that began, "'But enough of love,' said the laughing barber, 'Now I shall tell you of how the butterfly slew the ox.'"—and then another story with no clue as to how this tale within a tale began!"

The Emperor's eyelids fluttered. His pupils focused on the boy; and the boy, seeming to take courage, moved forward.

"I walked for a day in this cave, and climbed down a well where I traced more writing—more tales, branching into two, three, four others—or merging from multiple strands into one. There was a tunnel that went off into the dark. I crawled through it—it was very tight. But inside I found the story of a fisherman's wife, who returns home one day to discover a girl in a white gown who offers her a cup of tea. The fisherman's wife drinks. The girl withdraws. And later that day, the fisherman's wife is summoned to the tax-collector Jan-Yu. Her husband and four sons are crouching at the tax-collector's feet. Jan-Yu bids the woman say farewell to them, and decapitates them in her presence. The woman gathers the heads in a basket and departs.

"In one version of the story—for here the tale divides into two—the woman carries the basket with a chest-harness (after all, five heads can get pretty heavy), and goes down to the Yangtze to wash the blood from the heads before burial. But at the river's edge she finds five headless torsos sitting in the reeds, turning this way and that. She puts her husband's head on one, and it comes to life and scolds her for putting his head on the body of his weak son with the shriveled penis."

Here the courtiers laughed, and even the Emperor smiled.

"Of course, she can't remove the head once it's attached, but she's so happy to see her husband again that she sets to work at a brisk pace and brings the others to life as well. She tries her best, but in her excitable state she muddles and mismatches the heads with the bodies. Nevertheless, the family is restored and together they return and slay the evil tax-collector.

"But then the fisherman's wife finds herself in a real predicament. For now she must choose whether to have intercourse with her son with the shriveled penis (who now wears her husband's head), or with her husband's strong, lovely torso (now surmounted by the head of her slobbering idiot son)."

The Emperor leaned forward, and his face exuded curiosity.

"In another version of the same story, the tax-collector is justified in having slain the men, who were all evil, and the fisherman's wife—a witch!—the worst of the lot. To avenge their deaths, she shaves the hair from the heads, rips out her fingernails, casts the whole mess in a bowl and chants. And after that, no matter what Jan-Yu puts in his mouth to eat, it turns to hair and fingernails. But the tax-collector's daughter, a clever girl, saves her father by poisoning the fisherman's wife."

Here the muleteer's son paused, advanced to within an arm's length of the Emperor (a presumption unprecedented in the imperial annals), and spoke again: "And this, Son of Heaven, is the most extraordinary part of all. For at this point the writing in the tunnel straggled up and then backwards over my head. It arced over to the opposite wall, wound back down and went under my tummy, and linked up far behind me at the very beginning of the story where a beautiful girl in white offers the fisherman's wife a cup of tea...It's Jan-Yu's daughter slipping the witch the poison, you see?"

The Emperor's eyes twinkled and his face radiated satisfaction, and with a turn of his head he wordlessly dismissed the assembly, so that he might deliberate with himself how to proceed. Geographers and surveyors were appointed to interrogate the muleteer and determine with precision the cave's location. The muleteer was given sacks of copper and granted land in a remote commandery at the foot of the Great Wall, and he and his son were sent on their way.

As the mule-cart lumbered off, the palace servants swept the spaces behind the wheels to purge the stone flags of the pollution occasioned by the visitors' presence. The muleteer's son turned to look behind him; and the Emperor, in the distance, seemed no more than a gleaming point winged round by thousands. The boy bestowed on the Son of Heaven a half-smile and faraway look that in the windless, cloudless afternoon seemed at once a farewell, a benediction, and a curse.

The cave's mouth was made wide, and the statue of Jum-Sum extracted and removed to the palace, where it was placed in the royal gardens and a lofty pagoda raised over it. A university was established at the mountain's base, and a broad hypostyle linked it to the cave.

Here the empire's greatest scholars convened to systematize into books the stories that had been retrieved from within. It was a process that exhausted some and drove others to despair. Men hanged themselves in the rafters or commanded subordinates to run them through with swords when they contemplated the impossibility of gathering into a single indexed register these fragmentary and partial tales that often had no beginning or end.

All round the green mountain's flanks, houses, barracks, dining halls, and hostelries were erected to lodge and feed the scholars, soldiers, and imperial emissaries who abided or sojourned there. The Emperor endowed one hundred thousand calligraphers, and furnished them with lacquered brushes and porcelain ink-pots. Scaffolding and duckboard filled the cave; and railed steps ascended and descended its interior. Here men puzzled over doubtful glyphs that time had obscured or nature had partially effaced.

Each day the chief librarian sent couriers on swift horses to the imperial palace, their saddlebags bursting with scrolls containing the fruit of the university's researches. A court of academicians sorted and arranged the tales at the palace to ensure the Emperor was always provided with the choicest of them for his delectation. A numeric value was assigned to each story, so that if one rated 1,234 in degree of wondrousness arrived at the palace after one rated only 1,233, then the former was presented to the Emperor before the latter, lest (that is) an even more magnificent and pleasing tale overtook the twain in transit.

Attendants read the tales to the Emperor as he paced the palace grounds or was massaged at night. Sometimes, with gloved hands, the Emperor read the stories himself and admired the paintings that filled the margins between the text.

One day when the Emperor was still a young man, the imperial suite was interrupted as it processed towards the pagoda of Jum-Sum. An old woman with bleeding lips emerged from the fumigated precincts and crossed a stone bridge spanning a lily-pad pond. She drew herself up before the gathering of men and sneered.

The chief minister quieted the myopic official who had been reading aloud the story of the falling star that sank into the sea and was eaten by Aomen Tai-Tai, the haughty oyster who mistook it for a pearl and flaunted it over her sisters.

When the reader stopped, the minister advanced and addressed the crone: "Who are you that would disturb the Emperor's ease?"

The woman growled and shook her head. When she spoke it was in a hissing, ugly voice.

"No Emperor is he, for Heaven has withdrawn its Mandate. He has violated my sanctuary and plundered my treasure house; the mine is stripped of its ore. Thus says Jum-Sum: Nevermore shall the Emperor dream, nor will he ever sire children, for these are the things he has taken from me."

The Emperor furrowed his brow but said nothing. The woman was seized and put to death, and from thenceforth prophecy and the casting of oracle bones were proscribed throughout the empire.

The Son of Heaven did not take the old woman's words to heart. True, he could never remember his dreams after that, but that did not mean that he did not have them. Sometimes he thought he had dreamt one thing or another, but on reflection it turned out to be a story he had heard or read long ago. And although none of his concubines or wives conceived, he regarded it as a slight thing, for he had always known he would be the last of his line, and had decided long ago that he would rather spend his waking hours diverted by strange tales than waste his days attending to affairs of state or teaching a sniveling brat how to govern, and rule, and be adored.

As the years passed the empire grew frail at its edges. Territories were lost to marauders or taxed into poverty to sustain the Emperor's grand enterprise. The university launched expeditions far into the depths of the cave that were either never heard from again, or whose remains were discovered when yet another team stumbled upon the former's bones and baggage. Some of these unlucky travelers recorded their tribulations in the gaps between the writings on the walls. Others had taken an abundance of paper, ink and lamp oil along, and had left sheaves, covered on both sides with tales they had retrieved from chambers even deeper within the cave.

One autumn afternoon a bearded man emerged from the cave's entrance, shielding his eyes from the declining sun. He wandered without aim through the university's cloisters, walking over the red leaves that lay between the red pillars. Three doctors were summoned and looked gravely at the man and gravely at one another, and pronounced him to be about thirty-five years of age.

The man spoke beautifully and in the classical style. He claimed his mother and father had journeyed into the cave when the university's paint was new. He had been born and reared in a subterranean world miles beneath the mountain, a land perpetually lit by phosphor and replete with freshwater lakes and deep-plunging cataracts. Here he and his parents lived off blindfish and glowing fungi, but because they knew no change of seasons, they could not mark time. And so the boy, who was now a man, did not know his own age. But the man's mind was nimble and retentive, and his parents had taught him to read, and had enjoined him to memorize the tales that lined the walls in the region of the cave they inhabited. And so the man, who was believed to be about thirty-five years of age, brought with him 35,000 unrecorded tales and some of their variants.

❋   ❋   ❋

"I am dying," said the Emperor in his 90th year, "and would see my tomb before I am gathered unto my ancestors."

The attendants bowed and withdrew from the colonnaded balcony. The Emperor placed one hand on the balustrade, and peered out into the middle distance where the pagoda of Jum-Sum, lit from within, loomed high over the royal gardens. Pale lightening quivered overhead, and though it was dark and growing darker, the Emperor could see thick columns of black smoke rising beyond the walls of the imperial city from the war-blighted land.

The covered chair bearing the Emperor passed through the pillar-gate, and, in a driving rain, descended the steep, flinty trail that led down into the Gorge of Shades. Ledge dropped to ledge, and fell to foaming rapids below. The roads had grown dangerous in the tide of unrest that swept through the land. Footpads and cut-throats had formed communes, and lay in wait for easy prey. And so the Emperor's captains issued directives and established dispositions to secure the route, so that the Son of Heaven's progress might remain unembarrassed.

A towered stronghold midway down the gorge guarded the dynasty's tombs. The covered chair passed under the stronghold's portcullis and was settled on the courtyard's flags. One wall of the stronghold was a cliff, covered with straggling vines. A coin-shaped slab, vast and wide, had been rolled aside, exposing the mouth of the catacombs. The Son of Heaven's way was pavilioned with hides to shield him from the slanting rain. Unbending from the chair, he trod on dry carpet to the threshold of the tomb.

It would have been a sacrilege for a mortal to accompany him within, so the chief minister proffered a lantern with bowed head. The Emperor found the lantern's heft cumbrous, but the novelty of exerting himself in holding it pleased him. Courtiers, eunuchs, soldiers, seneschals, and dignitaries filled the courtyard and lined the path up and out of the Gorge of Shades.

The Emperor entered the tomb. Galleries opened to the left and to the right, but the Emperor moved forward into yet another gallery with an even higher ceiling. Rounding a corner, he passed the sarcophagi of his forefathers and paused to contemplate his own. It was shaped like a little house, with a double-sloped roof and pilasters on each façade. Next to it was a paunched likeness of himself, sculpted some ten years before.

The walls were paneled in rosewood. The Emperor remembered his father having brought him here as a child to show him the secret treasure room where each of his predecessors had deposited an artifact dear and peculiar to him. Two dragons locked in combat were carved in a medallion before him. The Emperor pressed the upper dragon's eyes, and a door creaked inward and shook dust from the jamb.

The Emperor stepped through and descended a ramp that sloped gradually downwards into the treasure room. It was here that the founder of the dynasty had left his suit of armor. Here the Emperor's father had left his curved sword. One ancestor had left a long model of a junk with coral inlay to symbolize his dominion of the sea. The most melancholy relic of all was a bronze baby-rattle that had been crusted in verdigris when the Emperor had seen it as a child. There was a strange tale behind it.

The child emperor Bai-Yu died before his first year. The tiny corpse was stitched into a burial suit of white jade. The death mask had neither eyes nor mouth, but merely a slight protuberance to suggest where the nose had been. The empress dowager was inconsolable and refused to part with the body, even when the flesh grew putrid. At night she whispered to it, cooed at it, or shook the rattle over it.

Time passed, and a new emperor was chosen from the cadet branch of the family, who confined the mad dowager to a remote suite of apartments in the corner of the imperial city, so that she might live out her days in peace. And the body of Bai-Yu was interred here in the catacombs. But one winter's night, when fierce winds beat the walls and snow swiveled through the alleys and streets, the empress dowager disappeared.

The following day men heard a sound like the clink of jasper beads on a horse's harness, and followed it some twenty li into the cedars. They found her seated in a clearing, ice-needles hanging overhead. Her pink gown stretched unruffled to the tree line and not a single flake of snow rested on the fabric. In her arms was cradled the body of Bai-Yu. She had pried the mask from the infant's burial suit, and its lipless mouth clung to her lifeless breast. In her free hand she held the rattle, which clinked in the gusts of wind like the sound of ice forming at a river's edge, like jasper beads tinkling on a horse's harness.

The Emperor thought on this as he descended the ramp. He patted a bag of Quanzhou satin that hung from his belt. In the bag was a scroll he intended to leave in the treasure room as a consummation of his reign. It was a book he himself had authored in which he had digested and epitomized the choicest of the stories he had heard and read over the course of his long life. At the end of each story he had appended observations on its import and wisdom, interspersing these essays with gnomic poems of his own invention.

But when the Son of Heaven reached the foot of the ramp and spread the lantern's light on the treasure room's walls, he was appalled to discover the room empty. Nothing remained. Robbers had excavated a tunnel into the treasure room and had carried off each and every one of its artifacts. The tunnel, tall and smooth at the edges, had been scooped out of the living rock.

The Emperor peered into it and was about to turn away, when he noticed a blood-dark smudge out of the corner of his eye. He raised his lantern so that he could see it more clearly. And what he thought had been a stain, he knew now to be a brushstroke forming a character, and beside it were more characters forming sentences, and phrases that trailed off into the dark. And then the Emperor smiled and stepped into the tunnel, and read:

The Tale of the Fifteen Doll-Makers

Once long ago in the Kingdom of Han a noble and prosperous family died in a conflagration that consumed their entire estate. The family's serfs and relatives were aggrieved, and commissioned an association of doll-makers in a distant province to fashion likenesses of each member of the family to inter in the burial vault, since neither bone nor tooth had been recovered from the scorched ruin.

Fifteen doll-makers worked fifteen days, and each produced a magnificent doll corresponding to one of the deceased: there was one for the mother, one for the father, one for the grand-mamma, one for the grand-papa, and eleven for the children of varying ages. The dolls were sealed in tong-wood boxes, and the lids covered over with charms and wards to consecrate their contents. And the doll-makers set off along a road that passed through a dismal swamp to deliver the dolls to those who had commissioned them.

But they soon found themselves lost. Their pack animals got stuck in the mire, sank, and died. And so the doll-makers carried the doll-boxes over their heads, for the water sometimes reached to their chins. They despaired of ever finding their way out, and when they rested on a mound of mud that night, they wept when they considered their plight. But their leader raised their spirits with these words...

Here the story split in two, and the Emperor read the lower thread:

"Cheer up," he said, "for I find our situation not unlike that of the dwarf who rode a bamboo-framed kite into the mouth of a volcano, and landed on a ship of ice bobbing in a flaming sea."

At this point the thread slithered sidelong down the wall passing under the Emperor's knees, and disappeared into a hole in the floor from which a sluggish rat emerged and waddled past his feet. The Emperor grimaced, and went back to follow the upper thread:

But their leader raised their spirits with these words: "Gentlemen, between those gnarled trees in the distance I see lights hung in tiers, which must betoken a place of habitation. Thither let us bend our steps and see what there is to see."

And so the doll-makers advanced through the muck and spongy ground, and came to an opening where a three-storied mansion rose high overhead. Vines had climbed up its walls and hung impleached from the flaring eaves. The structure leaned drunken to one side, and its foundation had sunk deep into the sludge. The front steps were flanked by stone turtles covered with black moss. But within there was light, so the men climbed the steps and passed through the doors which stood wide open.

An old man and his wife, both blind, greeted them in the antechamber and presented them with warm clothes and padded slippers. They conducted them to a room where a table, covered with steaming bowls of rice and savory meats, awaited them. Fruits were heaped on the board, and earthenware cups brimmed with delicious wine. The doll-makers ate and drank their fill. They thanked the man and woman, who beamed at them and seemed pleased by their presence. "Our host welcomes you," the man said, and rose from his seat to walk over to a canopied couch at the far end of the room. The man drew a tasseled cord. And the canopy parted to disclose a grisly sight.

Stretched on the bolsters lay a skeleton dressed in the robes of high office and crowned with a scholar's cap. The skeleton held a frayed writing brush poised over a piece of paper.

"Behold," the man said, "Your host, the Mandarin Tzu-Kung." The doll-makers were astonished and turned to one another in bewilderment, touching their temples to signify their doubt in the blind couple's sanity.

Throughout the meal, the man and woman would stop from time to time to address the skeleton, saying things like "Yes, Mandarin" or "How clever you are, Your Excellency" or "We are at your service, Sir, and shall do as you bid"—all the while turning their glaucous eyes on the doll-makers, grinning and nodding affably.

The doll-makers maintained an air of aloof courtesy and asked the couple how they could ever repay them for their help. "For we should surely have perished," their leader said, "had you not rescued us. But we must not tarry for long, for we are under a commission and must fulfill an obligation that has been entrusted to us. But we are lost and know not the way out of this wretched swamp."

"The Mandarin Tzu-Kung assures you he will supply you with all the food and drink you need," the old man said. "He will provide you with a map to guide you out of the swamp, but in return he would be entertained."

"How so?" asked the doll-maker's leader.

"You have brought dolls," said the woman, who leaned into the table's light. "Tzu-Kung loves to watch puppets caper and dance, and mime the stories of old."

"What you ask of us," the doll-maker's leader responded, "we cannot do; for we are craftsman, not entertainers. And the dolls we bring with us are sacred things. They are to be placed in the tomb of a family whose restless spirits roam the smoke and fog between worlds. For us to desecrate these dolls and make them toys for this worthy gentleman were a harsh thing indeed." Here the *leader wafted his hand at the skeleton and winked wryly at his colleagues, knowing full well that the blind couple could not see him. But the recumbent skeleton, whose robes stirred in the draft, seemed to grin down on him.*

"Nevertheless," the old man said, guiding the fifteen doll-makers to their room, "the Mandarin would be entertained."

That night the men lay side-by-side in a sturdy, broad bed with their feet sticking out from under the blanket. Their leader, who lay in the center, addressed them in a whisper. "The man and woman are clearly mad, but we are grateful for their hospitality and must honor their grey hairs. But tomorrow we depart." The others assented, and with that the fifteen doll-makers closed their eyes and were blessed with gift of sleep.

But in the morning when the men awoke, one of them screamed and pointed, for there in their midst lay their leader stark dead, his hair white, his skin grey and shriveled. The fourteen remaining doll-makers sprang from the bed. And seven of them knocked their knees together and made water; and the other seven knocked their knees together and made dirt.

Here the Emperor emitted a wheezy laugh, and leaned against the wall with one hand.

The men trembled and clung to one another, as the old man and woman entered the room in apparent disregard of what had happened. The woman placed a pitcher of water on a stand near the basin. And the man clapped his hands and said, "The Mandarin extends his greetings to the fourteen doll-makers. He wishes to inform them that a workshop has been fitted out for them, furnished with tools, so that they can transform the dolls into puppets. No expense will be spared."

And here the woman joined her husband at the door and finished his speech, "But the Mandarin would be entertained."

Now the wisest of the doll-makers was also the most venerable, and his name was Lao-Jia. He had a thin white beard but no hair on his head. A monk had taught him to read when he was a boy, and he had learned by heart the 300 Odes and had studied with interest the Five Classics. But it was a trove of stories locked away in a governor's yamen that had pleased him the most. The governor had granted Lao-Jia access to the books. Lao-Jia had read them and re-read them, and had recounted what he had read to the governor and to his family until the tedium of his voice had driven the governor to banish Lao-Jia from his house. Unlike the other doll-makers, Lao-Jia had traveled far and wide. He had transformed a hollow log that overhung a pond into a hermitage, where for twenty years he had communed with the tutelary dragon that slumbered beneath the water.

And now seeing his colleagues in this plight, Lao-Jia addressed them thus: "Brothers, I fear we will end up stark dead like our leader if we ignore the couple's words. I propose we humor them to save ourselves. Let us make the dolls dance. Let us entertain the Mandarin's ghost. My head is full of stories and I am ready to draw out a yarn or two if it will rescue us. What do you say?"

The doll-makers assented and with one accord submitted themselves to Lao-Jia's management.

The tong-wood boxes were opened, and some heard the dead family sigh; others claimed to have seen weeping shadows behind the rice-paper walls. Soon the little dolls were being mutilated and modified to make them limber enough to stoop at the knees and waggle their heads in jest. The arms were snapped off and refastened with hooks and twine. Meanwhile, landscape scenes were painted and beasts and wild demons were made of paper and adorned with baubles, ribbons and beads.One doll-maker could play the bridged zither, and others had musical acquisitions that their brothers knew nothing of, but which they now set out to improve by practice and rehearsal. Two months passed and the doll-makers stood ready to present their show.

The fog outside had seeped into the room where the stage was set. Tasseled lanterns dangled here and there between the cobwebs. But it was the glowing joss-sticks standing upright in the sand-bowls at the foot of the Mandarin's couch that tranced the room and lent the whole event an atmosphere that was unutterably funereal.

"And now," said Lao-Jia lifting his hands, and bowing to the Mandarin, "we present to you the most magnificent stories ever told." The blind couple applauded from the shadows. And the other doll-makers, clad in black robes with veiled hoods, readied themselves in the platforms overhead or positioned themselves around the stage with props and instruments. The bridged zither sounded and was accompanied by the clack of resonant stones, and Lao-Jia spoke again.

Here the story branched into seven separate tales, and the Emperor lifted his lamp to the first one, which began with the words, *"We begin with the tale of the thumb-tall woman, who hid in her husband's beard and thereby discovered his infidelity."*

The Emperor considered pursuing this thread, but decided to check the other stories, just in case they were more interesting. The next was about a cobbler who

made shoes for footless men—a tale the Emperor predict-
ed would 'limp along' without aim. The third story was
about the riddling boulder of the Tarim Basin, which the
Emperor recalled having heard before—or at least one
version of it, so he passed over it. But when the Emperor
came to the fourth story, his eyes expanded in wonder;
and he smiled and leaned closer to the wall, and read on:

*"I shall now relate to you the story of the Cave of
Branching Tales." The doll-makers let down onto the
stage a poor man and boy in rugged clothing. A child doll
sat on the throne, looking very imperious, with its head
bobbing up and down. Lao-Jia continued: "Robed courtiers and eunuchs preceded and followed the muleteer and
his son, who were driven more than escorted into the audience chamber."*

Here the story went on. The Emperor knew the plot
very well, for he had lived it. But even this tale forked into two versions very early on. In one version the Emperor
executes the muleteer and his son, and orders the mouth
of the cave sealed off forever—*"And thus was Jum-Sum
appeased, and the Emperor lived a very long and fruitful
life, and sired 400 children."*
The Emperor stifled a yawn, and refused to pursue
the thread any further; besides, the text had intersected
with yet another story and had moved on into a new plot.
He backtracked, and resumed at the point that followed
most closely the course of his own life. In this version of
the story, the grand-mamma doll was the old crone with
bloody red lips and wild hair. The father doll was the
man who lived under the mountain, whom the doctors
estimated to be about 35 years of age.

As the Emperor read on the words climbed high over his head, until he could no longer read them. He raised the lantern and craned his neck. The thread ran along the ceiling, and then forked like painted lightening into three, four, five—and then twelve bands of text, which split suddenly from the boldest trunk overhead, and went each one down a separate corridor.

The Emperor followed one at random, but was brought to the ledge of a cliff. But the text continued overhead winding through the stalactites, splitting off into even more threads. He tried another way, and descended steps that came to a pool of still water with a seemingly infinite path of stepping stones trailing off into the distance, and decided not to go that way. At last he found a corridor, where the ground was smooth, and where the text above slithered back down to a level where he could read the words once more. And so he read on:

"And at last," Lao-Jia said, "He found a corridor, where the ground was smooth, and where the text above slithered back down to a level where he could read the words once more. And so he read on.

"Of course, the Son of Heaven never made it out of the cave.

"For three days and three nights the imperial retinue stood outside the royal catacombs in the unremitting rain. Men lining the path out of the Gorge of Shades fainted or expired, or tumbled headlong into the river below. But still they waited, and still the storm raged on. The wind sucked shut the door to the secret treasure room.

"And on the third day the chief minister, having overcome his trepidation, entered the catacombs, and re-emerged soon after to announce that the Son of Heaven

now supped with his ancestors. 'For,' the minister said, 'he has climbed into his own sepulcher, and by the supernatural might vouchsafed to him has closed the lid over its mouth.'

"No sooner had the chief minister spoken, than the rain ceased abruptly. The coin-shaped door was rolled once more over the mouth of the tomb. The imperial retinue passed through the stronghold's gate, and ascended the steep, flinty path that led up and out of the Gorge of Shades; and their brilliantly colored robes, though draggled, shone bright and splendid in the grey hush of the sunless dawn."

As Lao-Jia finished, he approached the couch of the Mandarin Tzu-Kung, and looked down at the paper beneath the Mandarin's frayed brush. He was surprised to note that where formerly the page had been blank, it was now covered with a map depicting the swamp as a bird might see it from the air. The mansion was clearly marked, and a bold line wound through the hazards and quagmires, and led out of the swamp and into the neighboring province.

And when Lao-Jia looked up, he was equally astonished to discover that the Mandarin's brush was no longer frayed, but was sleek with black ink, and the face of the skeleton was now covered with breathing flesh, though the eyes remained closed as if drowsing.

And so Lao-Jia dropped to one knee and raised his palms to the sky, for he knew he was in the presence of the divine.

Here the corridor became narrow, and the jagged walls tore at the Emperor's robes. He removed the candle from the lantern, because the light had grown dim and the lantern heavy. Sideways he pushed his bulk between the rock and felt his feet sink into the damp clay, but still he read on.

When the doll-maker Lao-Jia spoke again, he spoke quietly and in an unexpected manner, with a strange, cloying eloquence that surprised and at some remove intimidated everyone present.

"My father, the muleteer, died prosperous, happy, and full of years. Would the Emperor had been so fortunate. But the Son of Heaven had grown weak, cruel, and vain. His false estimation of his own merit had led him to set his worth above the gods. And so the Emperor perished...so to speak."

Lao-Jia smiled and shrugged his shoulders. "You see, he had grown a bit fat in his old age."

Here the grand-papa puppet descended from the scaffold above, and two doll-makers below trapped it between shields representing the cave's walls. The poor puppet shook and wriggled, as the bronze drums crashed and the bells pealed harsh and loud.

"Some say Jum-Sum had his final revenge on the Emperor; for not only is he the god of dreams, he is also the god of sleep. And as he had withdrawn the gift of dreams from the Emperor early on, so now he withdrew the gift of sleep. Trapped in the cave, the Emperor died in the body but his mind lived on forever, eternally vigilant, peering from empty sockets into the unrelenting night."

Lao-Jia stopped. And at that moment the eyes of the Mandarin Tzu-Kung, which is to say the eyes of Jum-Sum, snapped open, and the stage went dark.

The Emperor could no longer move. The hand holding the candle was pinned above him; and its flame, though not yet extinct, was sinking low into its wick. Tears coursed down his cheeks, and wax coursed down his arm. But even here the story divided, and one thread curled to the Emperor's right like a hawk's talon and read *"So ends the tale."* But the left thread coiled in on itself, with diminishing characters forming a perfect spiral with the center-point level to the Emperor's left eye. And so he read on:

"And that," said Lao-Jia, "is how the Emperor came to his end. Or so they say. But the other version I've heard, and the one I find most credible, is that the Emperor never existed at all, but was an invention of Jum-Sum's. And that his story, his choices, his failure, and his fate, lie hidden and undivulged somewhere deep in the nighted recesses of the Cave of Branching Tales."

Fragment of a 14ᵗʰ Century Persian Recension of a Lost 10ᵗʰ Century Arabic Biography of Eminent Philosophers of Baghdad

Sheikh Tahir 'Abd al-Hakim (fl. 831-848 C.E.)

IT HAS BEEN RELATED by Sheikh Abu-Ishaq 'Abd al-Karim al-Hurrani, who received it from the grammarian, Muhammad 'Abd al-Qadir al-Baghdadi, who said, "I overheard a young man, a Christian logician and translator from the House of Wisdom, address the philosopher, Tahir 'Abd al-Hakim, under a date tree near the mosque and say, 'O Sheikh Tahir, what is a similitude of the mind of God?'

Sheikh Tahir tapped the sand at his feet with his stick, and with the tip began to describe a circle but stopped, and wiped smooth the sand and said:

"The mind of God is like unto the greatest poem that was ever composed. The poem is not infinite, for then it would not be complete. It is self-contained and complete, but contains infinity within it. It is a poem so brief that it could be recited in less than fourteen breaths. It is a poem so intrinsically complex that neither its wording can be adjusted, nor its tone or meter altered; for then it would lose its capacity to generate images, pure forms, mathematical relations, time. Yet even though the poem is perfect and brief, it has been imperfectly translated into a thousand various tongues. It has been expanded, edited, and commented on by fools, such that its meaning has become obscure, its theme recursive, its burden contradictory. Moreover, the original poem has vanished, folded in upon itself in grief. It is forever unrecoverable by man, such that man must infer its splendor from the derivative translations, ancillary marginalia, bloated commentaries, scraps, and distortions that remain.

'I have recited this poem. Whether I have done so now or as I slept or woke between the confines of night and day, you must decide. That is a similitude of the mind of God.'

The young man seemed disappointed with this answer, and lowered his eyes to contemplate the place in the sand where the philosopher had blotted out the circle he had begun to trace. But when he looked up once more, Sheikh Tahir was nowhere to be seen, nor was he ever seen again. The young man was troubled in spirit, but he returned to the House of Wisdom and dutifully rendered the philosopher's words into the Greek tongue and into the Syriac tongue and into the Arabic tongue; but these versions have since perished.

The young man abandoned the Nazarene creed and entered into the faith of Islam. He assumed the name 'Abd al-Karim, and became known as Sheikh Abu-Ishaq 'Abd al-Karim al-Hurrani. And this I heard from the grammarian Muhammad 'Abd al-Qadir al-Baghdadi, who heard it from a young man, who once met the philosopher, Tahir 'Abd al-Hakim.

The White Hairs
of Black Wolf

*(Adapted from a late 19th Century
fable by Josef Popper-Lynkeus entitled
"Die weißen Haare des Lao-Tse")*

WITH THE BOY at his side, the young shaman Black Wolf walked over the grass along the blue stream. The boy marveled at the landscape, the wild azaleas, the spreading beeches, and said, "If the earth is so wondrous on the outside, how lovely it must be on the inside."

Black Wolf kicked the edge of a ravine, and a clump of sod slid down and exposed a riot of beetles, worms, and ants—each warring, one with the other. "Look, and see what's inside."

The Algonquin boy lowered his eyes, and Black Wolf spoke to him and said, "When you have gained in knowledge, you will not find such a thing astounding. And when you have gained in years, you will not find it melancholy."

Black Wolf returned to the tribe at sundown, and stepped into his wigwam, where a hickory fire was lit. A naked woman sat cross-legged on the brush bolster, her face and breasts so radiant that Black Wolf stood gaping at the threshold.

"Why do you not banish me from your dwelling?" she said.

And Black Wolf removed his dress and stood, glistening and handsome, in his loincloth.

"Why do you not ask me where I came from?" she said with a thin smile.

Black Wolf's eyes grew wide, and he said, "The Great All-Mother shines forth from your face. The life-giving principle of the Earth and all that's on it covers you as a mantle." Black Wolf touched his lower abdomen, felt his loins stir with lust. He dropped to his knees, and put his hands on her inner thighs. "I would see the wonders within you."

"Look, and see what's inside," she said, parting her face as a curtain. In each hand she held the flesh, like marsh weeds, between her fingers. Black Wolf saw the blood and sinews, saw the maggots and carrion, and sprang away in horror.

The woman closed the flesh and sat immobile as before. She regarded Black Wolf curiously, and the fire light dimmed down and died. And Black Wolf heard her voice in dark say, "When you have gained in knowledge, you will not find such a thing astounding. And when you have gained in years, you will not find it melancholy."

Black Wolf stepped from his wigwam. The tribe was gone, the trees leafless, and the landscape bare and cold. The hairs on his head were as white as the snow that blanketed the earth. His shriveled limbs trembled. But in the chambers of his heart there now glowed a warm and powerful light.

The Museum
of
Oblivion

"Life is warfare and a mere pilgrimage. Fame after life is no better than oblivion."

"As for praise, consider how many who once were much commended, are now already quite forgotten, yea they that commended them, how even they themselves are long since dead and gone."

(Meditations of Marcus Aurelius)

WE USE THE TERMS "envy" and "jealousy" interchangeably. But we envy those who have what we have not, and we are jealous of those who have what once was ours but is no more. The one I loved more than anything in this world was lost to me. For years I was "jealous" of my rival for having deprived me of what I held most dear; but I "envied" those qualities in my rival that lured my beloved away.

This species of envy and jealousy is seated in the faculty of Appetition; it is common to both man and animal. But there is a different kind of envy, a different kind of jealousy, one peculiar to man and located not in Appetition, but in Reason, in Memory, in Imagination. It is the envy and jealousy of the artist. A dog will "envy" a kennelmate the bone it has found; it will snarl "jealously" when its master heaps affection on another. But a poodle that has been taught to dance will neither critique another dog's performance, nor care if you tell it that its own technique is derivative and lacks originality. But a man will.

The Catalan architect Isidre Bartomeu erected the Museum of Oblivion to blot out from the memory of man the works of his hated compeer, Antoni Gaudí i Cornet.

I met Isidre Bartomeu in 1924, when he was in his seventies, and I but only seventeen. To describe my first meeting with him would be to describe every meeting thereafter. I was never his intimate, merely a young acquaintance, a hanger-on, a cypher. He lived in the coastal city of Cala de Sorra, south of Tarragona, and held court daily at the Dancing Moor Taberna in the heart of the city.

Isidre Bartomeu was a gigantic man who favored white linen suits. His mustachios, always waxed and curled, were the same color as his nicotine-stained teeth. Wiping sweat from his bald head, he would pass between the half-dozen marble-topped tables littered with his sketches. This was because the owner of the Dancing Moor prided himself on being Isidre Bartomeu's chiefest promoter; and Isidre reciprocated by transforming the taberna into a sort of public atelier, a brash move of almost carnivalesque self-aggrandizement.

There were always people there. It was an odd camarilla: grey-haired satellites, feuilletonists, young table-companions. They lounged in a haze of cigar smoke. They would pose questions to Isidre Bartomeu on the merits of other artists, or invite him to lecture spontaneously on the origin and evolution of his own technique. A stream of words would issue forth from the master's mouth, as he bent over a sketch to add a flourish to a building's facade or cross-hatch the shadows edging another. Then he would stand back and admire what he had done, as the auditors applauded the brilliance of his improvised and seemingly effortless monologue.

His constant companion was a slender woman named Margarida, who never wore a dress, only men's suits. She kept her hair close-cropped and parted to the side. She wore steel-rimmed glasses. She would have been a beautiful homosexual man, but, as it was, she was probably a homosexual woman. The only trace of femininity in her were the agate rings she wore on both hands, as if to forestall any would-be suitors that might think her unmarried but marriageable. Margarida wrote down all that Isidre Bartomeu said in a black notebook, coughing from time to time as she waved the smoke from her eyes.

Isidre was a harsh critic. The works of Gauguin he dismissed as the daubings that an unlettered potter might slap on his wares. When asked what he thought of Monet, he would look more intently at his own sketches, "Of course," he would say, "the colors are arresting, but that is all his paintings are, colored flecks of light; no form, no meaning." But it was for his arch-rival, the architect Antoni Gaudí, that Isidre Bartomeu reserved the full force of his wrath.

Usually it was a student, a callow aspirant, who dared to mention the name. "But what," the poor boy would ask, "is your opinion of Gaudí, the father of the Catalan—"

"It is *not* Gaudí, who is the father of the Catalan style!—But *I*, Isidre Bartomeu, who invented and perfected it!" And by way of proof he would point to a photograph of himself on the taberna wall from 1873, showing him in canvas hat and baggy trousers (was he always so stout?), standing in a field of termite mounds in Africa.

"The style for which Gaudí is praised," he would add, "is derived from the zoomorphic stacks of the Australian and African termite. The Barcelonan *fraud*, which is to say Gaudí, in a vain attempt to conceal his patent theft of my technique, adds dragons, tiled lizards, Art Nouveau mosaics—He fills his cornices with trumperies, throws in a few curly-cues, and has the temerity to call it original!—To call it *art*!"

During these outbursts, Margarida would sit up in her seat, and never seemed to weary of recording Isidre Bartomeu's words in her book, the scratch of the nib audible in the tense and embarrassing silence that followed.

I was permitted to leaf through the master's prints, and I must admit they were stunning. Many of the designs were of turrets, tapering at the summits like pillars of sand. The buildings were dimpled, undulant, with serpentine flutings and strange symmetries that seemed faintly, but intentionally, skewed.

Through wheedling and intimidation, Isidre Bartomeu had forced the municipal council of Cala de Sorra to adopt his designs for the renovation of the Plaça Central. The shopkeepers had no say in the matter. Within three years, the facades of all of the buildings facing the square were of a uniform buff color with pyrite mixed into the plaster. The effect was of a melting sand-castle that glinted as the sun played on it throughout the day.

His second achievement was the Avenue of Buttresses. Twelve buttresses seemed to leap from the buildings on either side of the road. It overarched the city's central tram. There was an article about it in a famous French magazine, accompanied by a photograph of Isidre Bartolomeu during the ribbon-cutting ceremony, one hand on his heart as the other rejects the Spanish Architectural Award that the official from Madrid begs him to accept. Above all else, Isidre Bartomeu was a proud nationalist and advocate of Catalan independence.

An unusual feature of the Avenue of Buttresses was that each morning the arches were replenished with a quantity of sand that sifted through hidden sieves, creating the illusion that the arches were themselves vanishing in the wind. This was a source of annoyance to the tram conductors and passengers, who could hear the gravel-ping pelting the tops of the tramcars as they rolled under the arches. Pedestrians grumbled when the winds gusted the granules into their eyes and noses. But few complained, since the Avenue of Buttresses was an indisputable work of genius and a source of profound civic and cultural pride.

It is said that when Isidre Bartomeu learned in 1883 that Gaudí had assumed the responsibility of finishing the design and layout of the Sagrada Família Church in Barcelona, he collapsed in the streets of Cala de Sorra, foamed at the mouth, called Gaudí a sacrilegious showman, and, in a vision, saw his revenge in an even grander scheme, which was to be the erection of the Museum of Oblivion. Ground was not broken for the museum until the spring of 1900, and its expense (and the vastness and scope of its design) delayed and, at times, idled its construction altogether throughout the first two decades of this century.

All but the central rotunda was completed when my family came to Cala de Sorra in 1924. And I happened to be in the Dancing Moor that afternoon in 1926, when a man sprinted into the taberna to report that Antoni Gaudí had been struck by a tram and was dead.

"Good!" Isidre Bartomeu shouted, and his face grew red, his eyes widened, and he touched his right temple. And then he stumbled against a table, overturning it and its contents. The marble table-top cracked. Sketches of the Museum of Oblivion tumbled to the floor. "It is just that it ends this way," he whispered and collapsed. He had had a stroke. He had survived, but the doctor reported that he would be dead within the week.

Isidre was paralyzed from the neck down and could no longer speak. But Margarida, his devoted companion, could read in his dimming eyes his last wish. She stood at his bedside in the hospital and said, "It is his desire to die in the central rotunda of the Museum of Oblivion. He wishes to be buried beneath the plinth of the Sand-Man Colossus that will be raised over him. It is the museum's final and crowning piece; its design and specifications are in my possession."

"It's true," the owner of the Dancing Moor said. "I have Isidre Bartomeu's last will and testament. He has left all to Margarida, and appointed her executrix of his estate and of all his outstanding projects." And Isidre Bartomeu smiled from his bed, and tears coursed down his eyes.

There was a broad well in the museum's central rotunda as deep as a man is tall. Vats of concrete were being mixed at the well's edge to pour into the well once Isidre Bartomeu had died. At the bottom of the well was a strange death bed, part reinforced coffin, with a lid propped against the side to seal it shut and make a hollow caisson out of it. Margarida stood beside Isidre, who was propped up enough to accept the Last Rites.

The priest unfolded a portable table near the bed, lit a candle and opened his book. Behind him, an acolyte held the cup for the Last Communion and another the Eucharist. But when the priest walked over to the bed, Isidre Bartomeu's eyes glazed over and he died.

The priest sighed and shrugged, snapped the book shut, then, feeling ashamed, reopened it, and went through the motions of the Last Rites, bending his ear to Isidre's face, pretending to hear a confession that never came, touching the dead lips with the Cup of Communion and the Viaticum.

After the priest, his acolytes, and the other mourners had departed, Margarida stood immobile beside the corpse for an hour. And then, touching Isidre Bartomeu's brow, she turned and ascended the steps leading out of the well. One man remained, who fastened the lid over the corpse. Then the vats were tipped and the concrete poured in.

The Museum of Oblivion opened the following year. The great Colossus of the Sand-Man rose 24 meters under the stained-glass dome. The statue's fingers seemed to emit streams of sand that melted into the edge of the dome. A close examination of the strange reliefs carved into the rotunda's walls would have revealed an image of Gaudí's Sagrada Família disappearing beneath the rising dunes.

The Museum was like nothing anyone had ever seen. No one had anticipated it would be so successful.

In a shadowy room, hung with Nepalese thuribles, orange-robed monks, from midnight until sunrise, prepared gorgeous mandalas that were effaced when the museum's doors swung open for the day.

There were galleries filled with paintings, drawn not from things the artists had remembered, but from things they had forgotten. Items recovered from Roman and Phoenician tombs filled vitrines and display cases, but only those artifacts whose purpose none could fathom.

There was a library containing medieval manuscripts, uncials scraped from the vellum pages, a palimpsest entirely obliterated or overlaid with the text of an unmemorable Book of Hours. There were letters from the Napoleonic era, the ink of which had run, smearing the pages. Some visitors fancied they could read the uncertain scrawl (mere shadows of legibility), and infer meaning where no meaning remained: a soldier's optimistic letter to his mother on the eve of his death, an admission to murder, a suicide's last note, which he places in his pocket, knowing it will be destroyed when he plunges into the swollen river below.

The rooms and the galleries moved on wheels and tracks, or were hoisted or lowered to different floors, so that there was never an accurate map or plan of the museum's interior. There were secret doors and panels that would part, disclosing objects or entire rooms that had been transferred from one end of the museum to the other. Isidre Bartomeu had done this because he knew that just as mutability is the agent of memory, so is it its annihilator.

The eccentric Dalí i Domènech ambiguously praised the museum when he called it "The greatest chamber of marvels that the 20th century will soon forget."

One display was a modernist tableau formed from the hats and umbrellas previous visitors to the museum had left behind. Contemplating this and other wonders within, newcomers often unwittingly contributed to the display's aggrandizement by leaving their own umbrellas and hats at the garderobe upon departure.

Somewhere in the museum's depths you would have come to a room with marble steps rising to a mock stage, flanked by ionic columns. At the top of the steps was a vast relief of a kneeling actor, hair tumbling over his bowed head. The figure's muscular arms, outspread like those of the chained Prometheus, or the wings of a vulture, held in one hand the mask of Tragedy, and in the other the mask of Comedy. The mouths of the masks formed doorways into two unconnected tunnels.

The tunnels were lined with photographs and daguer--reotypes. You would have not been surprised to see the

Hall of Tragedy filled with images of death: mass executions in Bohemia, a beloved Crown Prince lying in state, tubercular children being lowered into coal mines. Nor would you have found it odd that in the Hall of Comedy there were black-and-white scenes of marriages, christenings, boating trips. But sometimes the pictures of infants in Comedy were accompanied by photographs of grieving families standing over a tiny grave. And in the Hall of Tragedy there were images of bodies mangled in the trenches of Verdun juxtaposed to photographs of young athletes hoisting trophies.

I once asked Margarida why Isidre Bartomeu had created this misanthropic exhibit, which had nothing to do with forgetfulness. "On the contrary," she said, "it is fitting for the Museum of Oblivion; because it shows us a truth that we all know but that we willingly forget, which is that all happiness is tinged with grief, and all misfortune, no matter how great or private, is a source of dark amusement to at least one other, perhaps to God."

But even the Halls of Tragedy and Comedy were never the same. And if you were to visit the museum a second time, you would find yourself in another part of the edifice, emerging from what you thought had been the Hall of Tragedy or the Hall of Comedy from your first visit, only to find yourself emptied out into the room with the marble steps rising up to the mock stage and the massive statue of the actor holding the masks in either hand.

I can attest that the Museum was disorienting. And I believe in my heart that there was something supernatural about it, but I can not quite recall what feature or aspect made it seem that way to me. Nor have I memory of how my memory was drained off by its effects.

❋ ❋ ❋

The Museum lasted less than five years. The expense to maintain it was too great. There were the three electrical generators, the grease for the wheels of the mobile rooms. There were pulleys and winches, not to mention the staff that numbered in the hundreds: janitors, engineers, curators. The trustees kept raising the ticket prices until only the wealthy could afford to visit. And then, one day, the trustees of the Museum of Oblivion simply forgot to pay the staff. The lights were extinguished, the doors chained shut, and the building stood hollow and empty for several years.

The entire city of Cala de Sorra fell on hard times. The shop owners, the barbers, all the proprietors who had set up business in the Plaça Central, abandoned their establishments because of an ordinance mandating that no advertisement or identifying signs could be placed on shop fronts or doors, since this would have blighted the aesthetic unity of Isidre Bartomeu's facades. And so the rented spaces fronting the square were vacated, except for three municipal bureaus and a disreputable bank that transacted with the cronies of Italy's Mussolini.

And then tragedy struck Cala de Sorra in 1935 when a massive earthquake struck. The Plaça Central was shaken and much of the plaster on its facade fell away. The Avenue of Buttresses was severely affected, one arch crashing down onto a tram car, killing four people, including the conductor. After that, the mayor ordered that all twelve arches be dismantled for public safety.

But what happened to the Museum of Oblivion was cataclysmic. The stained-glass dome over the rotunda shattered, many of the walls collapsed, the Colossus of the Sand-Man toppled and fell, and a rift opened into the plinth on which it had stood. And what was truly weird is that the caisson in which Isidre Bartomeu had been buried was exposed and gaped open, but the body was nowhere to be found. After that, the museum acquired an evil reputation. It became a hissing place, cursed and avoided.

When the Spanish Civil War broke out the following year, some of the heaviest fighting was seen in the streets of Cala de Sorra, and many of its walls were peppered with bullet holes or destroyed by artillery shells. The citizenry fled the violence, many left as refugees for France. The city became a ghost town. It has been said that an entire platoon of Franco's men entered the Museum of Oblivion to garrison there, but simply disappeared and were never heard from again.

It was not until 1967 that I saw Cala de Sorra again. I had not planned to go there, but the cab driver stopped near an abandoned train depot to relieve himself. When he returned I stepped from the cab and told him that I would be back in an hour. The driver grinned and snicked on his meter. And so I leaned in through the window and gave him some pesetas and told him he could leave.

"But Señor," he said. "There is no one around. And the town you asked me to take you to is still twenty kilometers away."

"I'll find my way back," I said. And so he drove off.

I passed through the rail yard, with its rusting cars on the sidings, and came to that single road that led down to Cala de Sorra and to the sea. The road was pot-holed and cracked, but I was not prepared for the scene of desolation that met me. The buildings were sunk in sand. Telephone poles tilted this way and that, the wires gone, probably stolen. And the sea had advanced into the city itself. There were buildings and rubble lapped in foam.

In the distance I saw where the Museum of Oblivion had once stood. It was no longer walled, but, near the edge of the water, a vast circle, like a great arena, marked the outline of what had been its central rotunda. I descended the road, and was surprised to see a wisp of smoke rising from a hole in the rotunda's center. For twenty minutes I walked, sometimes over uncertain terrain, my feet sinking in the sand-drifts.

I reached the rotunda. There were piles of gutted fish and eviscerated seagulls close by. The stench was oppressive. I approached the hole that had once been covered by the plinth of the Sand-Man, and, coming up out of it, was a bent creature. Her hair was wild and grey, she wore rags. She threw on the ground the remains of a crustacean she had been chewing raw. Had I not seen the agate rings on her chapped fingers, I would not have recognized her.

"Margarida," I said, but she did not know her own name. "What are you doing here? This place is unhealthy. And you are old."

When she spoke, her voice was like the voice of one unused to speech. "I am waiting for him to return," she said. And then I saw her pinpoint pupils, and knew that I was in the presence of an amnesiac.

"Whom are you waiting for?" I asked.

"For the man who built this place," she said, as an apartment building collapsed in the distance and was swept into the sea.

"If you mean Isidre Bartomeu, he is gone. He died long ago."

She looked at me, pityingly, and walked away.

It was pointless to remain; I could not help her. I turned and left Cala de Sorra, passing automobiles sunk to the door-handles in sand. All that remained of the Avenue of Buttresses were its iron supports rising like tusks from the shifting landscape.

I began this narrative by quoting the words of Marcus Aurelius, that reluctant and philosophic emperor, who would likely have found it surprising that his stray *Meditations*, composed under the duress of war, had not perished with him, but were still read and admired. I climbed the road by which I had come, and his words recurred to me: "As in the seaside, whatsoever was before to be seen is by the continual succession of new heaps of sand cast up, one upon another, soon hid and covered; so in this life, all former things by those which immediately succeed."

I looked down one last time upon the ruins of the Museum of Oblivion, and upon the vanishing city of Cala de Sorra (The Cove Sand), and I turned my back on them, and knew them no more.

POSTSCRIPT

I FOUND THIS REMINISCENCE *in a small box in an antique shop in Madrid. The vendor sold me the box and its contents for 20 euros. The box had a label written in Catalan that read simply "Things to Be Forgotten".*

In the box I found some photographs and a small notebook with this story in it. The first photograph was of a young man, whom I presumed to be the author. He was seated alone in the Dancing Moor Taberna sometime in the 1920s. There were photographs of him with a friend his age. In one they are hiking in the sierras. In another they are on a beach in bathing suits. I could tell that they were in love. There was one photograph from the time of the Spanish Civil War, and they are both in uniform, the author is sitting beneath a rocky overhang, sharing his blanket with his friend, whose hand has been bandaged and who rests his head on his lap. And then there was the crumpled photograph. It is from 1942, and the author's sad eyes stare wanly from it; he is in a suit, and his beloved friend stands next to him, a bride at his arm. The last of the photographs was taken in the early 1990s. It is a retirement home for men; there are seven of them in it, but I can not find the young man in the faces of the old.

If you were to look on a map for Cala de Sorra, you would be hard pressed to find it. The sands and the wasting sea have long since done their work. But if you travel some 320 kilometers northeast along the coast from where it once stood, you will pass through Tarragona, and you will come to the city of Barcelona—a city designed for the making of memories; where the men and women are proud but welcoming, where the young are amorous, and where the elderly sit on the benches of the long avenues, their hands on their canes, and recount with unerring exactitude the stories of their youth. Walk along the beach, and you will see a sunset that will haunt you at sunrise in your waking dreams. Nor can you forget—for how could you?—that from one end of Barcelona to the other, the city is overlaid, dotted, and adorned with the magnificent works of that incomparable artist and father of the Catalan style, Antoni Gaudí i Cornet.

A Styrian Horror Story

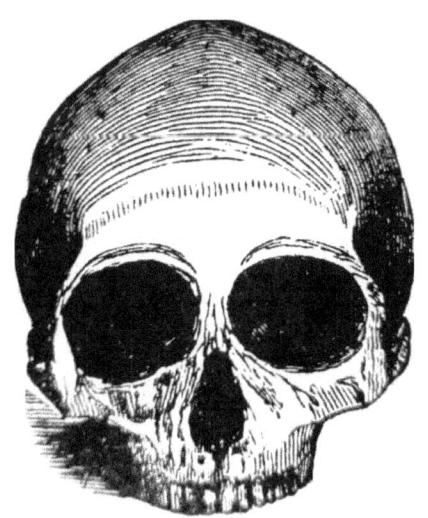

IN THE TOWN OF BRUCK an der Mur in Styria, long ago in 1627, a remarkable incident happened. Three murderous highwaymen were caught and condemned to death. They had killed nine Christians, possibly more.

The youngest, Ernst Offenbach, a lad of 14 years, said he had been forced into brigandage by the other two, who had killed his parents and hoisted him from his crib when he was an infant. The Burgomeister, who sat in judgment, was deaf to the boy's entreaties. And on All Saints Eve, when the colored trees rose gorgeous out of the valley, he ordered the three hanged from a gibbet near the mill. Their bodies were to be given over to the butcher, Ruprecht Schinder, to be cut up and fed to the sows.

63

The women of the town were told to stay home. And the three malefactors, two bearded men and a beardless boy, were made to stand on wooden stumps, with a rope cinched round their necks. Their trousers were slit at the back, per Ruprecht Schindler's request, because he did not want to cart the bodies to his shambles if the pants were soiled and stank from the dirt the three would issue at death.

The priest performed the last rite, held a wooden cross before each, and prayed for their souls, although he said it was doubtful they would escape Hellfire. The ropes were the length of an ell. The miller walked over with a mallet and knocked the stumps out from underneath each one; and the three kicked in the wind until they were dead. At sundown, the miller cut the ropes. The bodies tumbled to the earth and were heaved into the cart. And Ruprecht Schindler trundled off to his home.

He called his sons, they helped him move the bodies to the shed. A cow hung from a hook. He had the bodies propped up against the wall, and told his sons that he would chop them up on the morrow.

There was a wind and a strange growling sound that woke Ruprecht in the night. He looked outside, and saw a black wolf enter the shed. He grabbed his blunderbuss and ran from the house, shouting and yelling. The wolf darted from the shed, sprang over the paling and was gone.

Ruprecht went back into the house, lit a tallow candle, and returned to the shed. He trembled at what he saw.

The two elder corpses were no longer bearded. Their faces were smooth, and the grey dugs hanging to their waists proved them to have been women. Their hands lay at their sides, as if they had fallen slack after embracing the beloved. The corpse of the boy was nowhere to be seen. It was only when Ruprecht looked into the hollow of the cow's belly, where its tripes and guts had been, that he saw the body of Ernst Offenbach curled up with his hands pressed together in prayer.

When Ruprecht made his account to the Burgomeister and the priest, they ordered the bodies of the hags burned, but pardoned the soul of young Ernst Offenbach, and buried him in the churchyard with a cross at his head.

They say that on All Saints Eve, when the wind whips hard through the valley of Bruck an der Mur, you can sometimes see two naked women sprinting through darkness pursued by a boy angel flogging them.

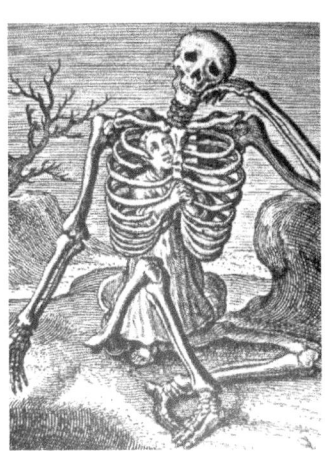

The Mirror of Solomon

SOLOMON PLUCKED ME from the ceiling of a vault where I hung by my ankles, blind and bat-like, shrieking with my brothers in the night. And by his keys he locked me in a body of polished copper, flat, smooth, and round. I never saw my own frame, but I have been told it was forged with great cunning. It was crowned with two rams' heads facing each and terminated in sea-beasts' tails intertwined. My name, which I knew not, was incised in rude Hebrew characters about my haft, and was legible only to sages, magi, and priests.

"Furthermore," Solomon told me, "on the day you hear your name, you shall surely die."

I was a prized treasure and ornament in the Temple of Solomon. Hidden away from the eyes of the profane, I was consulted by men of understanding. I shadowed forth for them forms and images—wheat fields bending to the blasts of storms, the crumbling towers of foreign cities; the subversion of the great, the raising of the low, the decollated heads of prophets, wives, and weak-willed kings.

When I was carried off into captivity in the city of Babylon the Great, I despaired of ever serving man again. But I came into the hands of a powerful seer, who wore a chain of office in the court of Balthazar. The dreams of others he could interpret, but not his own—or so he told me. And so he looked into me "as in a glass darkly," he would say, and smile, and I suspected that he mocked me, and that he already knew what he sought from me—or at least in part.

I was lost, sold, seized, or given away to others throughout the years. I ended up in the possession of a woman of vanity, who used me merely to admire herself. When her bark was dismasted by high winds on the Sea of Galilee, the mariners used me to signal by the sun's rays another boat. I cannot remember whether we were rescued by merchants or plundered by pirates, nor do I care. I never saw my mistress again; and thereafter my life grew tedious.

Again I dangled upside-down, hanging from the nails of shops or the crossbeams of itinerant peddlers. I grew bored and disregarded my surroundings. Like the slurred tale told by a drunkard, I cared not how it ended.

But then one day I woke as from a trance. Someone had spoken to me.

"Your name I will tell you, Servant of Solomon." I could not see the man who had spoken, yet I felt his hand gripping the haft on which my name was incised. I could see his shadows wavering on the walls of his hut in the glow of the oil lamp on the table beside him. But I could not see his form, nor was his face reflected within me. "Your purpose is spent," he said. "The one whose advent you foretold and whose miracles you prefigured is come. By subtle thaumaturgy, Solomon drew you from the realms of night to fulfill the will of the Most High. But the Son of Man walks among us now. I too was dead, but am reborn to sojourn for a term until I am recalled to the mansions of twilight. But though I live again, I live not as I was. Your name I know; for it is even my own. And I feel a strange sympathy for you, and a desire to free you from your captivity. And therefore sleep, Lazarus, sleep."

A great sadness fell upon me. Tears sprang into my eyes, forming patinated stains that marred all my splendor and well-wrought beauty. Instantly I crusted over with filth, grime, and soot. I became a thing ugly and misshapen, a porous lump, neither metal nor stone.

Dust covered me. I was buried. And above my head was sown a seed of the Fruit of the Tree of the Knowledge of Life-in-Death. I slept centuries in a moment, a dreaming heart, prisoned in the ribcage of fibrous roots that netted me round, until that day when I woke at the voice of one who spoke to me, but in a whisper, and whose name means "God is with Us".

"Awake, Lazarus."

I opened my eyes, which were become crystals, beaming forth far-seeing rays of light. I spread wide my wings of feathered adamantine. And when I soared, up-risen, above a land of polished glass, of silver mountains, and vast, still seas of unruffled waters beneath a sky of perpetual day, I saw, and, in seeing, knew that I had been reborn into a world of surfaces that reflected all things as they truly are, a world in which I, too, Lazarus, Servant of Solomon, was mirrored forth into eternity and perceived by a greater and all-seeing eye.

The Feast of
Saint Christopher

THREE WEEKS AGO, at the end of June 1941, the Russians withdrew from the Galician town of Lwów. That day, Abram Rutenberg was returning home with his grandson. The boy Lev held cordwood that Abram had bought for the stove. As they emerged from the alley, Abram saw members of the German Einsatzgruppe standing on boxes, filming and laughing as Ukrainian nationalists whipped naked Jewish men and women through a gauntlet of jeering Christians.

Lev dropped the wood.

Abram saw his granddaughter stretched dead on the street, his son-in-law herded into a truck, and his daughter sitting naked in a pool of her own blood, her breasts on her belly, her pubic hair matted with gore. She saw her father and in an instant, an act so subtle that only Abram noticed, she begged him to save Lev and flee; and then fearing that if her gaze lingered on them too long it would alert the attention of the mob, she turned her face to the man clubbing her to death and closed her eyes.

Abram grabbed Lev by the collar, pulled him back into the alley. He walked as swiftly as age would permit, and opened the rear door to the dry-goods warehouse that he owned. No one was there. He sat his grandson on a crate, fell to his knees, and said, "Your sister and parents are gone. Take this money, it's all I have. You are nineteen and strong. Leave the city through the Plotva sewers. You must find a job as a farm laborer. Your name is Casmir Hazjusz, and you are a Christian. Repeat it."

"Casmir Hazjusz," the boy said.

Abram grabbed a pair of scissors from a peg, removed his wide-brimmed hat and cut his forelocks. Then he went to the boy and said, "We can't be seen together. But I will always be with you." And then he cut Lev's forelocks, and a tear fell from the boy's eye.

Less than an hour ago, they had left the woodcutter's yard. The boy had plucked a wild marigold from the ground, put it jauntily in his coat pocket, and then put the wood down and pretended to propose to a girl and proffer the flower to her. Abram had laughed at the boy's antics, had even laughed as a motorcade of Mercedes with Nazi flags snapping at the headlights had passed. Now Lev removed the marigold from his pocket, crushed it in his fist, gave it to his grandfather, and sobbed.

Abram kissed the boy's cheek, and the two left the shop through the same door by which they had come in. Lev sprinted down the alley to an unfrequented street with access to the Plotva sewers. Abram walked in a different direction towards the limits of the city. He had decided to walk back to his shtetl, either to die where he had been born, or on the way there, if he were detained.

But Jan Majnek, the tobacconist, saw him coming up the cobbles near the medieval gate and stopped him.

"You and I have known each other for a long time, Abram Rutenberg. We've watched our children grow together, and together watched our wives waste away with cancer. You can sleep in my storeroom. You'll sweep the floor, pretend you work there. We'll say you're a cousin from Danzig, since you're fluent in German. It may work, it may not." Jan concluded each sentence with a shrug, as if it didn't really matter how it all ended. "No one knows you on this side of town, Abram Rutenberg. You should be safe."

"Thank you, Jan Majnek. That is very kind of you. I will accept your offer." That was three weeks ago, and now it was 24 July.

At one forty-five in the afternoon, the shop-bell rang, and four Germans came in. Their leader seemed no older than his grandson. Abram took the broom from the wall and started sweeping the floor. The leader pointed to Abram, and laughed. "There's an old geezer if ever I've seen one." And he turned to Jan and said, "Why do you have such a useless old fellow like that working here?"

Jan could not understand German and shrugged.

"He's a—how do you say? A 'stary chelovek', that one is," and laughed. And the others laughed too, but Jan just looked at him.

"Gerhardt," said one of the soldiers, "you didn't finish telling how you found the Jew."

Gerhardt smiled, and looked into the empty jars of the tobacconist's shop, and said, "Oh, yes. It was on a wheat farm, just outside of town. It was this morning. The laborers were about to depart to the fields. I asked to see their papers. The farmer produced his and I laughed, and said I knew he was a kulak, but that I was curious about the others. I told him we would search his workers' personal effects. I ordered the laborers to stand in a line. We went into their sleeping quarters. It didn't take long. I found the Jew's papers in his kit: Lev something."

Abram went into the storeroom and sat on a burlap bag, the broom still in his hand. He listened as the soldier, whose name was Gerhardt, went on.

"I came out of the cabin, and walked in front of them. I didn't have to say anything. The one called Lev fell to his knees."

"Did he cry like a Jewish dog?"

"No," Gerhardt said, and his voice sounded faint. He faltered, but only for a moment, and then he said in a quiet voice, "No, he didn't. He never cried. He just turned his head and looked at a marigold growing at the fence post, and I shot him."

The Germans laughed, and Abram turned and peered around the corner. Gerhardt was looking straight at him, but did not seem to see him.

"Do you at least have matches?" one of the soldiers asked Jan. But Jan could not understand him and shrugged. "Fucking Pole," the soldier said, and bought a Turkish blend of tobacco from Odessa that was dry, and walked out. The others followed, Gerhardt last.

"He paid more than it was worth. It is two o'clock in the afternoon," Jan Majnek said. "No one else will come today. I will close the shop. Goodbye, Abram Rutenberg."

"Goodbye," Abram said.

Jan patted Abram on the shoulder, and said, "One day this will pass. And we will do business again, like old times." And then he locked up the shop, and was gone. Abram sat alone in the storeroom for an hour, then unlocked the door, stepped out, locked it up again, and left Lwów for good.

The sun would not set for hours. Abram walked out of the medieval gate, no one stopped him. The occupying forces were absorbed in their maps, compasses, and logistical reports. Members of the Ukrainian Nationalist Movement were already being appointed to administer the city. The Germans were pushing further east, and the bombs of the Luftwaffe planes could be heard beyond the horizon.

Lev found an obscure path through the woods. It ran along a tributary of the Plotva. He found a long stick to support his weight. He stopped twice to rest; and, as the sun was setting around eight thirty in the evening, he came to the wooden Catholic church that stood opposite his shtetl on the banks of the stream. The church's three onion domes and sloping roof were covered with green moss.

Abram decided to go into the church before crossing the stream to the shtetl where his father's home and the synagogue had stood. He saw two men in cassocks lying dead on the porch. The rails that supported the overhang, the walls, the doorjamb---all were cracked and splintered from machine-gun fire. There were still candles lit inside, and a niche to the side of the altar was aglow. The attack must have happened recently.

Abram sat down at the back of the church in a wooden pew, the *prie-dieu* at his shins. He felt a tightness in his breast, which passed. He sat there for hours, until shortly before midnight. And then he heard a faint gasp, hoisted himself up with his walking stick, and went to the niche. It wasn't a niche, but a small shrine. An icon of the Virgin looked down over a sand-filled pan of candles.

On the floor lay a woman. She had evidently been unconscious, and was only now waking in a swoon. She looked up at him. In her arms was a nine-month-old boy sleeping. The woman's face was contorted in agony, but the child was strangely quiet. She lifted the child to Abram and cried out, a stain of blood stretched from her armpit to her abdomen.

Abram accepted the baby and said, "I'll take him to my village and find him a home."

The woman nodded and closed her eyes, and soon expired.

Abram placed the child on his shoulder, and the babe clung to his head. He could feel the infant's warmth, feel its breath at his ear. He left the church and walked down to the edge of the stream. He knew the shallows, knew how the rocks lay, where the stream's bed buckled or dropped down. He stepped into the water, which rose to his knees, and, probing his way with his walking stick, began to ford the stream.

The German soldier Gerhardt sat on a rock at the edge of the water, studying the effects of the moonlight on a marigold growing from a rotting log. It was the Eve of the Feast of St. Christopher. His grandmother had given him a medallion with the Saint's image on it before his departure to the Eastern Front. And then she had kissed him on his forehead, and prayed for his safe return.

Gerhardt's right hand trembled; he held the Luger with which he had shot the boy this morning. He would throw the pistol into the stream, be done with it. It had dehumanized him: the pistol, his position in the Schutz-staffel, the war. What bothered him most was that he had enjoyed the momentary God-like power he had held over the life of a fellow human being. And he could still recall the tragic thrill he had felt when he had snuffed that life out. This was the Sin of Cain, which he had been taught to abhor from childhood, but which, in his weakness, he had embraced.

Gerhardt rose from the rock; and was on the verge of throwing the pistol into the water, when he saw it; the shadow of a man crossing the stream, receding away from him, with an infant at his shoulder. And the infant seemed to glow with an unearthly light. "If you see an image of St. Christopher," his grandmother had said, "You cannot die that day."

"There is no atonement for what I have done. I commit my soul to God," Gerhardt said, and put the muzzle to his temple and fired.

The infant turned and extended his hand towards the man who had shot himself on the shore, a gesture of either surpassing grief or casual redemption. Abram did not hear the shot; he had died hours before, sitting alone in the church. Abram found the child heavy—as if he bore the weight of the world on his shoulders, and yet his legs were steady, his pace sure, and a strength coursed through him that made the burden seem light. Nor did he find it strange that, although it was nearing midnight, the misty tree-line on the approaching bank was already shot through with the horizontal glimmer of dawn.

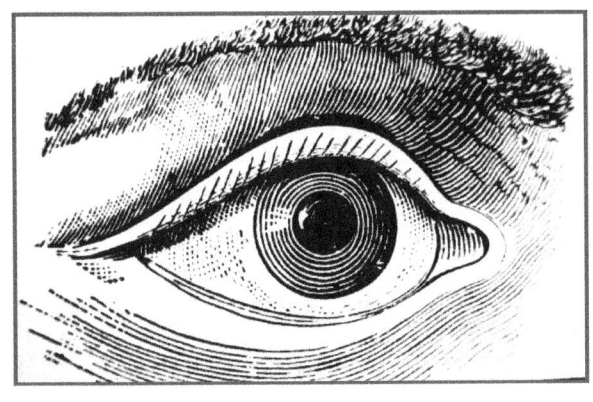

A Preliminary Hearing

A CORRIDOR LINED with black file cabinets trailed into obscurity in both directions. Pale light-bulbs, some winking, some dying, hung from the groined gothic ceiling overhead. The cords of the light-bulbs trembled when the crows clung to them in mid-flight to peer down at the spectacle below.

Grave men in black fedoras and blazers, women in dark business suits, sometimes singly, sometimes in groups, would stop at one of the file cabinets. A drawer would open, and the heavy rumble would echo through the hall amid the coughs and whispers of the other investigating magistrates.

If two or more stood together, one would hold a flashlight, so that the tabs of the manila folders could be read. There was one man who stood alone, a penlight between his teeth, rifling impatiently through the folders, pulling sheaves out and stacking them on the files of an adjacent drawer he had opened for the sole purpose of making it into a temporary shelf.

Elizabeth, in her plain grey uniform, could see down from one of the many barred windows that filled the upper galleries. She saw the black file cabinets and the investigating magistrates.

Each drawer in each cabinet corresponded to a single dead soul. But the files did not summarize what the soul had accomplished. Rather, each contained a précis of what the soul had hoped to do but never did. All the aspirations that remained unfulfilled, the plans unachieved, the talents and skills wasted—all dreams that withered away or were suppressed.

Some of the drawers were nearly empty, with only one or two files shoved to the very back of the cabinet. These belonged to children.

One drawer opened onto a grove in the early evening, with fireflies winking in the mist, and, in the distance, a small cabin with a curl of smoke rising from it. The magistrate peered down into it, scowled, and made a note.

Another drawer opened onto a beach at sunrise with a lover's face turned to the wind. And when the sun's rays poured from the drawer and lit up this bleak quarter of the hall, the other investigating magistrates regarded their colleague with a sour look, as if he had committed a public disgrace.

There were drawers with small terrestrial globes to represent that comprehensive dominion of the world that remained forever beyond the grasp of the foolish and the vain. There were drawers filled with money, gold, deeds, and stocks. Sweet cello music, an original composition never performed, poured from an open drawer somewhere far down the hall.

A corpse of a nagging wife, horribly mutilated, lay stretched inside one of the drawers between the bloody files. But the real wife died peacefully in bed next to the same meek man, who had spent the last twelve years of their marriage thinking of the most brutal ways to kill her.

One of the magistrates lifted a small leather notebook filled with numbers and symbols from a drawer. It was a mathematical equation whose application in the field of biochemistry could have extended the natural life of man by twenty years. And the two magistrates looked at each other and shook their heads, and the one who had lifted it from the drawer put it back in and sighed.

In yet another drawer, an old woman with streaming grey hair played "Ring Around the Rosie" in a field of dandelions. And when she collapsed, her classmates tickled her shriveled sides. And the woman laughed and screamed for sheer joy. The female magistrate, whose hair was wound in a bun, smirked and scribbled on her clipboard, and then slammed the drawer shut and the boom filled the vaulted corridor.

There were lurid scenes in some drawers, photographs and video tapes of men and women staring wantonly at the viewer, or lying naked on rumpled sheets. And the magistrates would merely take note in a clinical fashion, without laughing or even remarking; for to have done so would have been unprofessional.

One drawer opened, and a little pink baby whose eyes had not yet opened, was lifted from it. And one of the female magistrates began to sob, and the infant cried out, and with its frail fingers brushed the chin of the man that held it. "But she couldn't bear children," the female magistrate said. "Yes," the man replied, and solemnly lowered the child, which had always been hoped for but had never been born, back into the drawer. "But that's really immaterial to the case, don't you think?"

Elizabeth knew that the magistrates were collecting evidence, and had been doing so for some time. Others were incarcerated with her in these spacious interlocking cells, awaiting their preliminary hearings.

Some sat together at tables, playing cards, forgetting who had laid down the ace of hearts or the jack of clubs, forgetting even what the rules of the game were. There was a madmen chained to a bed, who turned to stare at her as she passed by.

But what was this place? The lines of Milton came back to her:

And that one talent which is death to hide
Lodged with me useless, though my soul more bent
Therewith to serve my maker and present
My true account.

Elizabeth spoke the words under her breath, and walked into another communal cell, and sat down on a couch in front of a TV that showed only static.

The *only* thing she knew about her situation is that neither she nor any of the others could fathom how it would end. Why were they being investigated? And why were they being tried? Would the outcome be punishment, reward, appeal to a higher court, or release? And if it were release, what would they be released into? She knew she was dead, but she did not know how long she had been in detention.

Surely the authorities were reasonable enough to draw a distinction between never having used one's talents, and never having accomplished that which lay beyond one's capacity and resources to achieve. And what of wayward fancies and never-never lands? Was it a crime to withdraw into one's mind and imagination? For that matter, what of cruel and wicked persons? What of those who sought greatness at the expense of others? Was ambition a fault, or was it a virtue in this strange annex of Purgatory? What of revenge and vindictiveness? If one turned down the prospect of raising one's station, knowing that in so doing it would have entailed another's loss or misfortune, would this make one guilty? Elizabeth shuddered, and an uneasy feeling crept over her when she considered that many great states, many institutions, societies, and holy orders were themselves founded on rapine, murder, and bloodshed.

Elizabeth reached over to turn the channel, and was surprised to hear the warden call her name. Two guards escorted her down a flight of steps and into a room with a single gunmetal-grey desk in the middle. A bald man sat at the desk, the lenses of his steel-rimmed glasses reflecting the beams of the goose-necked lamp that shone on her open file. The guards directed her to sit across from the man, and then withdrew. The door slammed and was locked.

"This is a preliminary hearing," the man said, and removed his glasses and wiped them. "It's a very curious case. Perhaps the most curious one I've ever come across."

Elizabeth rested her palms on her knees and looked straight ahead.

"You knew about this place. You dreamt of it. You saw the corridor, the file cabinets, the contents of the files. You saw the investigating magistrates, the other prisoners. You even saw yourself sitting here across from me."

And here the man picked up his pen and tapped a paragraph on her dossier. "And yet you never shared what you had seen, you never reported it, never wrote it down, never bothered to tell the story. But you often thought about doing so, and wondered whether it might not be the right thing to do."

He scratched behind one ear. "It wouldn't have taken much time, really. And the suspicion that you should have done so before it was too late occurred to you again, and again, and again...But you never did it." The man spread his arms, breathed in deeply, then placed both hands on the table. "And now you're here. As I said, it's a rather curious case. I don't think I need to tell you any more details, you already know them...But how do we proceed?" he said, and twinkled at her in an almost kindly way, pausing to let it all sink in.

Elizabeth felt her throat tighten, and tears welled in her eyes. But she didn't answer. It would have been pointless to do so.

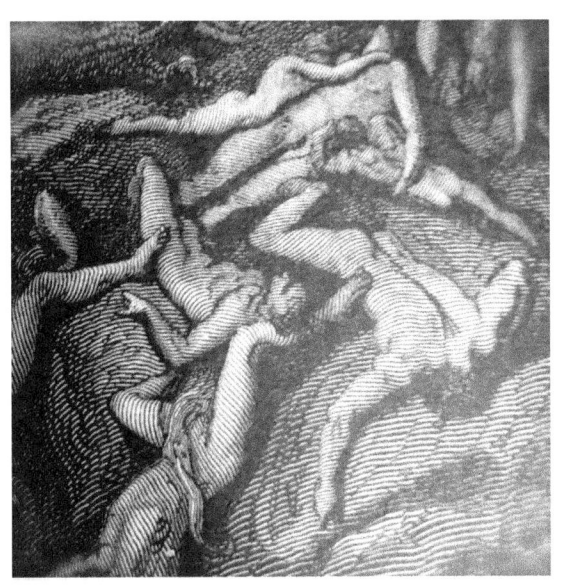

The Altar of
Aphrodite

HE SAT ON THE ROCK, one leg dangling in the water. His snow-white beard hung beneath his smile. He seemed relaxed and serene in the late afternoon sun. Eighty-five years lay behind him, but he was as spry as a kitten darting from the litter to bat at the afternoon's shadows.

It was not the face of a philosopher, nor Silenus; neither a king nor ancient god; but the face of a man at the close of his life, and in the fullness of his content.

His wife, white-haired, concentrated her chisel on the statue of him. The statue was identically posed and guarded the left of the tomb's entrance. The image was

97

marble and the steps of the tomb descended to the foam around her legs. The sea-fish nipped at her ankles but she ignored them. She chiseled at the statue's beard. *Clack-snick, clack-snick, clack-snick.*

He never regretted that she had surpassed him in the art he had taught her. He pulled funny faces. She smiled, and the wrinkles at her eyes tightened. She wore a corded soapstone tied around her hair to keep the strands from blowing in her eyes.

He looked at the tomb, and at the statue of himself. The green waters circled the tomb. All around them were hundreds of statues sunken, some to their chests, some only to their knees. Some seemed to be rescuing lambs in a flood.

Behind him soared a lofty wall of dressed stone that retained the sea, but just barely. And in front of him, high up—over the tomb, up the gleaming marble steps that rose to the brow of the mainland cliff, smoked the altar of Aphrodite.

The island quaked the night they wed, here on the westernmost crags of Cyprus. The earth sundered and gaped. They ran from his cottage, climbed up the hill. And at their feet was a basin, where the rock opened out of itself. A sheer wall held back the sea; it would give way some day, but not in one man's life. And there, heaped to the left and right, huge slabs of uncut marble.

"The gods have given us a wedding gift," he said. "It shall be our funereal garden, our death-house. Let us adorn it."

They found five flat stones. And at the top of the cliff, near a natural slope into the basin, they laid one stone on another until the five stood breast-high. And then they consecrated it to the goddess Aphrodite. They placed a bronze pan on it, and burned incense day and night.

They hewed steps out of the natural declivity. They carved friezes on the wall. Over time they graded the basin into ornate concentricities that narrowed into it. And in the wall that retained the sea, the woman sculpted a vast image of Dionysius twice the height of a man. Her husband was the model. It held a cup uplifted in one hand, and a sprig of grapes in the other.

One morning, late in his wife's first pregnancy, the man woke but could not find her. He climbed up the hill to the altar, and there she sat before it in the wild grass. The bronze pan had been thrown down. And on the altar lay a bloody heap in a white cloth. He knew she had lost the child. He sat down beside her.

"You did nothing wrong," he said. And he looked again at the upturned pan. "Nor did she." And then he drew her to him and hugged her, and said, "I wish you would let me help you lift this heaviness from your heart." And her voice was like the howl of a dying beast that, in anguished disbelief, cries out when a child prods it, laughing. He sat with her until the sun passed over their heads, over the death-house, over the seawall, and down into the sea.

At evening she rose, took the wrap from the altar, descended the steps, and set it in a niche. And then she rested her forehead against the rock until dawn.

The man woke to the sound of hammer-falls. He had slept on the grass by the altar. And now he saw that the pan had been restored, and smoked with incense. In the basin, over the niche where she had placed the stillborn, his wife was sculpting. For three days she worked. He brought her food and water, and she rested and took it. From her mind's eye, she carved her daughter as her daughter might have been, a nymph chased by a lover.

She never spoke of the loss.

The next summer she bore him a son. And, in thanks, carved a statue of Aphrodite from a slab of marble rising out of the waters at the base of the wall. The green sea had started to seep into the basin. The statue was on its back, one hand extended to the sky; and, as the figure was borne on the carved foam, the waters creaming its edges made it seem as if it were genuinely afloat.

The man's eyes began to dim; the stone dust had done its work. There was an overhang in the rock that he had shaped into the Nemean Lion, upheld by a muscular Herakles on the verge of throwing it to the ground. He knew he was losing his sight, because he could no longer discern the sinews in the deity's arms.

Now he spent his days at the top of the basin near the altar, while his wife worked below. He carved dolls. He made household gods and children's toys. And these he sold to the people in the village. And he made an ivory image of his wife, and kept it with him in the folds of his robe.

He helped when he could. The death-house stood on an island in the midst of the rising waters. He helped carve the steps, and smoothed its sides. He polished the columns of the portico that ringed it. And their adolescent son hollowed out the inner chamber that was to be their tomb. But the slab inside was narrow and could accommodate only one.

When the boy was grown and left, they were content with each other. Then one day a fissure formed over the statue of Dionysius, just over the uplifted cup. And when the sea rubbed high against the wall, the foam poured in and seemed to overflow the cup, cascading down the god's arm, falling in sheets over the chest and phallus.

"The time is near," she said.

And that was forty years ago.

Clack-snick, clack-snick, snick—snick—snick.

"It's done," she said, and dropped the tools, and removed the soapstone tie from her hair. And then she sat down on the steps, on the other side of the tomb's door, facing the statue she had just finished.

"I have done all the goddess asked of me." And she bowed her head. "No two have been, nor ever shall be, as fortunate as we."

He rose from the rock, and sat on the steps of the tomb, between her and the figure of himself.

"I'm ready," she said. And with that she rested her hands on her knees and turned to him. Her hair lifted in the breeze. He kissed her, and, at that instant, cold-white and smooth, the lips of Galatea were become marble. The fish still darted around her ankles, but none nipped at them now.

And Pygmalion rose from the steps, picked up an earthen cup, poured a draught of wine, and looked up at the cliff. At his back, the sun was sinking behind the crumbling wall. And before him, although he could no longer see the ledge clearly, high up over the basin and into the sky, rose a shadowy scratch, curling against the off-white remoteness of the dying summer's day. And he knew the altar smoked, and that the goddess heard.

He raised his cup. "That you answered my wish," he said, "I thank you. That you granted us prosperity and a long life together, I praise you for it." And with that, he sipped, poured out a libation, and cast the cup into the foam.

Pygmalion entered the tomb, and climbed up onto the narrow bier. From the folds of his dress, he drew the ivory image of Galatea, held it to his breast, turned his head to the right, and died.

Five stones stand on a cliff's ledge fronting the sea and the setting sun. Some say it is a landmark built by the ancients; others affirm that Venetian spies built it in 1571 to signal galleys off the coast when Famagusta fell. Today it is covered by a white-washed shelter, crowned by a blue Greek cross. Plexiglas covers its landward side, and there are icons hung on the five stones within. When the winds gust, the icons clack and the pane rattles in its frame.

Women come to pray that husbands, who have grown cold, will desire them once more. Old men, whose wives have died, pray that their spouses are granted peace, but beg for a companion to share the remains of their days. It is a tradition in the village for a boy and girl to burn a candle here on the eve of their wedding.

The locals have heard the theories. They have seen the tourists reading from guidebooks. It is a grave-marker, they say, a prehistoric cairn, a 19th century hoax (as evidenced by the inscription "Kenneth Craddock 1839" chiseled at its base). The locals smile, because they are indulgent. And they know it for what it is: a monument raised by two angels to be an altar and shrine to undying love.

The Retirement
of
Diocletian

"Diocletian's answer to Maximian is deservedly celebrated. He was solicited by that restless old man to resume the reins of government and the Imperial purple. He rejected this temptation with a smile of pity, calmly observing that, if he could show Maximian the cabbages which he had planted with his own hands at Salona, he should no longer be urged to relinquish the enjoyments of happiness for the pursuit of power."

(Edward Gibbon, *The Decline and Fall of the Roman Empire*)

M. Licinius Flaccus wishes the best of health to C.
Aulus Fabius, Protonotarius Imperalis.

The news has just reached us in Vindobona that Diocletian is dead. No one expected it, although we had
heard he was sick. What was the actual cause? We are
being told it was a perforated ulcer in his stomach.

Galerius has ordered the courts of Noricum, Panno-
nia, and Moesia into mourning, and the priests to make
elaborate sacrifices to him as a god, but no one is de-
ceived. True, Diocletian made him an Augustus, but Galerius was always, I believe, very much in the old man's
shadow.

As his protonotarius and long-time confidential secre-
tary, you once suggested to me that in fact Diocletian
knew what he was doing and, by virtue of *auctoritas*, was
still pulling the strings of both of the Augusti, Maximian
in Mediolanum, and Galerius in Nicomedia. You served
Diocletian for twenty-seven years. Do you miss him?

I am sure that he was up to more than growing prize
cabbages and seeking tranquility of mind. Even in retirement, were not both emperors mortally afraid of him?

Incidentally, his famous response to Maximian is now
alleged to have been delivered by Diocletian himself at
Carnuntum, during the great conference of the tetrarchs.
But I was there, as were you, and I do not recall the sub-
ject ever having been raised.

Valeria is said to be putting on a good show of grief,
and it may be sincere. Diocletian was a loving father, and
doted on her. But I have heard that she no longer comes
out in public, and rumor has it that she has some kind of
crippling disease.

I congratulate you on securing an estate near Rome and a nice stipend. May you live long to enjoy it. Will you be leaving Salona and the Palace of Spalatum? Do you plan to grow vegetables in retirement?

Farewell, Gaius, My old friend.

C. Aulus Fabius to M. Licinius Flaccus, greeting.

Your letter posted from the Grey Falcon Inn on the outskirts of Vindobona has arrived. That Diocletian's response to Maximian is rumored to have been delivered during the conference of the tetrarchs in Carnuntum, as you report, does not surprise me. But I assure you, Marcus, that as protonotarius, it was I who drafted the letter to Maximian, and the circumstances surrounding it are much more interesting than what has been let out.

I do not think it necessary that history be truthful to be of use. The words and deeds of great men should accord with the events they shaped and the destinies they fulfilled. Did Cincinnatus abandon the plow to fly to the aid of Rome? Or did he simply relegate the management of his farm to his slaves and bailiff? The latter is probable, the former appropriate.

Diocletian divided the empire into the East and West, and he appointed an Augustus over each. Titles and offices proliferated, taxes grew burdensome. And then he abdicated. And the peasant emperor from Illyrium withdrew to his estate at Salona on the Dalmatian coast to live out his days. But his wife Prisca stayed in Nicomedia, and none asked why.

The Palace of Spalatum, which was built for him, was grand. You and I, Marcus, have walked through the Forum to the Capitoline. Such was the palace's expanse in all directions. It was a fortress. Two garrisons were quartered there. On one side of the central peristyle was the mausoleum and on the other side, was the Temple of Jupiter, Diocletian's father.

I do not know if Diocletian believed himself to be divine. I had seen him smile tolerantly over the strange ceremonies of the Egyptians, who venerated him as a god. I would have thought him irreligious. And yet it was with fervor that he burned the Manichaeans at Carrhae. And his persecutions of the misguided followers of the Galilean Jew are notorious. Diocletian was a man of brutal efficiency, which is a quality that is often mistaken for deliberate cruelty. But did he think himself a god?

Before sunrise, I would attend him in his private chambers. It was his custom to sit in a rude chair, peering out of the only window that penetrated the defensive walls of Spalatum. As the sun rose, scattering the shadows in the fields, he would lift his palms, as if hoisting up the day, a gesture fitting for a god. Dalmatian mornings are lovely. And one time, as we watched the dawn progress, and as the sky grew pink and red, and the upcurling edges of the clouds took on the hues of the wild lavender at the window's edge, Diocletian said to me, "Do you know what time of the day it is?" I replied that I did not. "It is the time of the morning," he said, "when an emperor is most merciful."

An emissary from Mediolanum arrived by boat to deliver Maximian's message. A feast was held in his honor. Diocletian's daughter, Valeria, wife of Galerius, was visiting from the imperial estate at Sirmium. The emissary and other guests lay on couches, their heads in a half-circle around the lunette mensa. I stood at the door, but could hear the conversation, which was polite but frivolous. Valeria took up a plum, and said, "Taste this, father. It cuts the sharpness of Tragyrian cheeses." She extended the plum to her father and he took it but it slipped through his fingers. And one of the spotted dogs native to the region sprinted across the room and ate it under the mensa. Diocletian laughed, and shrugged helplessly. But there was more in that shrug than met the eye. The emissary from Mediolanum affirmed that Maximian was ready to share dominion with Diocletian again and restore the glory of the former empire. Diocletian said that he had read the letter, and that he would have a response on the morrow.

I accompanied him back to his room after the meal. We passed through the rotunda. Four statues in Syenaic marble stood in four niches around the room. Two represented the Augusti of the East and West; the other two were the Caesars. The dog that had eaten the plum was on its haunches in the center of the rotunda, whimpering. Diocletian knelt and stroked its head. He seemed crestfallen. And then he rose and told me to tell Valeria and the messenger that he would be pleased to walk with them in his garden before sunrise. I passed his orders to the slaves, and then I retired for the evening.

I went to the emperor's quarters early, when it was still dark. I found Diocletian dressed. The dog lay on its back on the floor, limbs frozen at crazy angles; it was dead. The guards met us with torches, some holding mattocks and spades. The emissary from Mediolanum and Valeria met us in the peristyle in the last watch of the night. We departed the palace through the Great Gate.

And as we walked over the hills, the stars began to fade. We entered the walled garden on the road to Salona. In the torchlight, I could make out row upon row of cabbages. There was a pool in the center of the garden with rank, standing water. The guards and I swatted at the mosquitoes that swarmed in profusion here. But do you know, Marcus, that the mosquitos, as if in recognition of Diocletian's majesty, left his person unmolested? The guards doused their torches in the pool's water. And we followed Diocletian, who passed deeper into the garden. It was discomforting, being assailed by bugs, but we dared not object or complain. I wondered why the pool had not been drained; it seemed to serve no purpose other than to breed insects and contagion.

Diocletian paused and took a mattock from a man close by. At once the sun rose and we could see what was around us. In this part of the garden, the cabbages were intermingled with human heads, rotting, bloated from mosquito bites. The victims had been buried to their necks. There were skulls, edged with leaves or covered with vines. At my feet were the dead and dying servants of last night's banquet. Diocletian prodded a rotting head close by, and it rolled to one side and bled maggots from the nose, mouth and eyes. Valeria bent at the waist and vomited. The sky flamed red and pink. Diocletian looked at the emissary from Mediolanum and said, "Do you know what the time of the day is?" The emissary looked uneasy, and said that he did not. "It is the time of the morning when an emperor is most merciful." Guards seized the emissary, forced him to his knees. He protested his innocence. Diocletian ignored him. "I am no longer an emperor," he said. Tongs were produced and the emissary's tongue was torn from his mouth. He screamed, but was gagged. Already the mosquitoes were settling on his face, clustering around his bleeding mouth. The guards tied him up, planted him feet first in the ground, and smoothed the dirt round his neck. Throughout all of this, Diocletian watched its effect on Valeria, who sweated and seemed as if she would faint, but never did. I stood in horror, and grew cold when Diocletian spoke directly to me, "Gaius Aulus, you will take a message." I lifted the wax tablet that I wore around my neck, and wrote:

"Diocletianus to M. Aurelius Valerius Maximianus:

"Your friend and former peer, whom you, Hercules, were wont to call Jupiter, greets you. My love for you is without bounds, but must be expressed within the limits of propriety, lest I betray the habits of the simple rube I was born, and which I have become again. I have received your letter in which you urge me to resume the title of Augustus and guide Rome through these vexatious times to restore Her to Her former glory. I am not unmindful of the love and esteem you hold for me, but if you were to see the cabbages I have cultivated here at Salona, you would not ask me to abandon this tranquility of mind for the pursuit of power."

We returned to the palace. And the following day, Diocletian saw his daughter to her carriage. She went to her knees and kissed his hand. And the carriage lumbered off over the rugged road to Sirmium, one hundred guards and servants in her train.

It was then that the cleansing of Diocletian's household began. The cooks, the servants, the grooms, all were escorted by soldiers over the Illyrian mountains to their death. Istrian mercenaries ambushed the soldiers as they returned from their commission, and put them too to the sword. Nor did the cats and livestock at Spalatum escape. For Diocletian feared that his enemies might cast spells and enchantments over the animals, and that they might act as agents against him. For the remainder of his life, he would suffer none but Istrians, Dalmatians, and a handful of Egyptian slaves to serve him, and guard his person.

I was sent in the emissary's boat to deliver the message to Maximian. But I did not know, Marcus, if I myself would make it back alive. I arrived in Mediolanum, was granted an audience, and read the letter to Maximian. He sat unmoved, and his advisers marveled at the virtues of this old man, who had rejected power, and who seemed to want nothing more but to end his days bent over his seedlings, like Cato between the Carthaginian Wars. I have often wondered what Maximian thought of Diocletian's response, and whether the disappearance of his emissary ever troubled him. All I know is that Maximian never reiterated his plea for Diocletian to return.

The old man sent me on a second embassy the following year. I traveled to Asia to deliver a message to Valeria, who was with her husband, Emperor Galerius of the East, and her mother, Prisca, in Nicomedia. Valeria's face was scarred, and she wore a veil. I stood before the three of them and spoke:

"From your father:

"Loving daughter, you grieve me. I know that it was you and Galerius who plotted to poison me, not the emissary from Maximian. I let the plum fall, because I sus-

*pected conspiracy but did not want to believe it. I lived
my life to advance yours. But you are willful, vain, and
foolish, as is your mother. When you returned to Sirmium, there was an Egyptian slave in your train, a maker of
cosmetics and perfumes. I commanded him to take away
your beauty. I will always love you, but I will not tolerate
disobedience from anyone, especially from a child of my
blood. And as for my son-in-law, whom I elevated to Augustus, I express nothing but contempt, scorn, and disap-
pointment. I realize that your husband fears me, and that
he thought my death would open his way to supreme
power over East and West, an idiotic idea at best. And I
also realize that you are a foolish woman, totally subservi-
ent to your worthless husband and his pathetic ambition."*

Galerius rose from his seat, and grabbed a dagger
close by. "Oudamos," Valeria said in Greek, and lowered
her veiled face. And by these three syllables, I was saved.
Prisca scowled at the floor, but did not otherwise react. I
returned to Spalatum, and sat with Diocletian over a
game of draughts the same evening that I arrived. He
never asked about my trip, nor did he seem curious as to
whether Valeria had responded, or how.

Not long ago, I was in Pola to notarize the sale of one
of Diocletian's estates. I returned by boat to Salona at
dusk and was met at the quay by three men who in-
formed me that Diocletian had died earlier that day. I
went to the palace and was admitted. Hired mourners
were scattered throughout the rooms and the alleys, gathered on the steps of the peristyle. They were grieving,
wailing, chanting dirges in unison.

I knew that I would have to put the estate in order before I could leave the Palace of Spalatum. There was a

knock at my door. An old woman with a blunt face and greasy neck stepped in. She spoke a garbled dialect of Greek, haltingly, and with the constitutional impudence of the lowborn.

"I have a message from Diocletian for you," she said. I gestured for her to sit down, but she remained standing. "I brought him his breakfast this morning. He was sitting up in his bed. I was about to leave, when he spoke and said, 'Mother, do you know what time of the day it is?' I said, 'It is the first hour of the morning.' He looked at me fixedly. I pointed at the red and pink sky through his window, and said, 'It is morning, nothing more.' I turned to leave and he said, 'Do not turn your back on me, I was once an emperor!' And I said 'Well, you aren't an emperor now, and you don't even look like one.' This amused him, he laughed. He said, 'Mother, do you know my servant, Gaius Aulus Fabius?' I told him that I did. He said, 'If the winds are opportune, he will arrive today from Pola. You will deliver this message to him. You will tell him, that he must dine this evening in my honor.' And then he looked at the tray of fruits and cheeses that I had brought him. And he said, 'And tell him that plums cut the sharpness of Tragyrian cheeses.' And then he smiled one of those half-smiles that he learned from the Romans. And I said, 'Will you dine with him?' And he said, 'Yes, but only as a god.' And I said, 'Sometimes you say things that make no sense to me.' And then I left. He ate his breakfast, and the stomach ailment he suffered from carried him off by noon."

I will never know, Marcus, why Diocletian took his own life, whether from despair, or in hope that in so doing he would preserve Valeria's. It is worth noting that Valeria never responded when I invited her to come to

Spalatum to mourn him. But Prisca his wife came, stayed a fortnight, and then returned to Nicomedia. Diocletian's Egyptian slaves were liberated and sent back to Alexandria. But the wording of Diocletian's will, on many points, is unclear, and so I have sent to Mediolanum, Sirmium, Pola, and Nicomedia for supporting documents. For example, nothing has been settled on the Illyrian servants and the Istrian mercenaries who remain here, nor do I have clear instructions on how the Palace of Spalatos is to be sold or disposed of.

You once asked me what kind of man Diocletian was. I served him for twenty-seven years. And I lived those twenty-seven years in fear. The lives of others were as inconsequential to him as the chaff dispersed by the wind. Make no mistake, Marcus, Diocletian was a deliberately cruel man, which is a quality that is often mistaken for brutal efficiency.

C. Aulus Fabius to M. Licinius Flaccus, greeting.

I have not heard from you in four years. I do not know if you are on the march, engaged in war, or dead. These are stirring times, Marcus, and my world has contracted. I am still at Spalatum. I am a hostage. I saw my freedoms erode gradually. It started when I tried to pass through a section of the palace leading to the former barracks. My way was barricaded. The mercenaries turned me back. They have become emboldened, have brought their whores, their wives, their children into the Palace. They stable in the stockrooms and baths; they sleep in the sculleries or on the flags of the peristyle. My role has become that of the guarantor of corn, which arrives regularly by boat. I sent messages to Galerius, and to notables in Mediolanum, seeking guidance on what I was to do, but no answers came. And now Galerius is dead.

A merchant from Calabria wrote to me, asking if he could visit Spalatum, he was considering buying it. I saw his ship in the harbor. I signaled to him. He answered. But then, perhaps fearing piracy or treachery, the boat simply went away. You have heard the parable of the man who bought a kingdom for a coin?—so worthless is Spalatum become.

When I walked along the palace jetty, I was attended by guards, who feared I might solicit the aid of a passing boat or bribe fishermen to take me away. One of my warders was a one-armed boy. I befriended him, taught him the rudiments of Greek. I even taught him how to read it. Because I could not pronounce his name, I called him Cyprian. But I dared not deceive him or recruit him to facilitate my escape, because I am certain he would inform on me. But I sent him on errands of business.

Each year Diocletian's death was commemorated at Spalatum on the anniversary of his passing. The Istrians and Illyrians painted their faces white, did strange dances through the courtyards and lanes. I was expected to participate in the procession. It was the only time in the year when I could pass through every quarter of the palace. The celebrants carried a wax effigy of Valeria at the front, because they worship her as the Virgin daughter of Jove. The festival would end with my dining alone in Diocletian's tomb.

But this year, something changed. You will have heard that agents of Licinius apprehended Valeria and

Prisca in Thessalonica. It is said that the mob could not tell which was the daughter and which the mother, until the women were stripped in the square and the smoothness of Valeria's skin beneath her clothes confirmed her to have been Diocletian's child. Both women were beheaded, and there was sport made of the severed heads, each one held over the other's torso, to mock how old Valeria's face seemed. When the news reached us at Spalatum, the crone who had waited on Diocletian in his last days came to me and said, "You were supposed to protect her." I spread my hands and asked her what it was that she had expected me to do. She did not answer. But this evening when the commemoration of Diocletian's death was held, no one painted their faces; there was no dancing, no train of mourner, no wax effigy of Valeria. I walked through the streets of Spalatum alone. I passed grim faces, and entered Diocletian's mausoleum, where the funeral banquet was laid out for me. I saluted the emperor's shade, and drank. And then the old woman shambled into the mausoleum, went up to the tomb of Diocletian, kissed her fingertips, and touched them to the sarcophagus. She looked at me coldly. I felt a slight pain in my sides, and knew that I had been poisoned, and that Diocletian from his grave had ordered that I be sent to my own. I am a Stoic, Marcus, and do not fear death.

I left the mausoleum, and saw the boy Cyprian, now a young man, crossing the peristyle near the Egyptian sphinx. I called him to me and said, "I have one last commission for you. You know the chest outside of my chamber door." He said that he did. "You will come to the room at dawn. You will find in it two scrolls and a bag of 1000 sesterces. One scroll is a letter to be delivered to the sister of my friend, Marcus Licinius Flaccus, in

Praeneste. The other scroll is a letter of accreditation. The sister of Flaccus will take you to my lawyer. You will present the letter to him, and you will be rewarded ten thousand fold what I give you tomorrow." His eyes bugged and he sprinted off. It was with some amusement that, arriving at my door, I saw him already sitting at the end of the corridor, his one arm flung over his knee. My room had formerly been Diocletian's. I lit tapers and sat down at the table to compose this letter to you. The pain is faint, but I have no doubt that it will turn to fire soon.

I wanted so much to see and embrace you one last time. How glib we are with the time allotted to us! How confident we are that tomorrow will always come. If you are alive, perhaps you will read this some day. If you are dead, then the two of us will soon share a laugh, as we harvest cabbages in the Elysian Fields. The stars are waning. I will close this letter. I have written and sealed the letter of accreditation. I will give both scrolls to my greedy messenger, who I am sure is even now leaning his one arm against the jamb. There was no point in my directing him to fetch them from the chest. When I have returned to my chamber, I will sit in the same chair that Diocletian was accustomed to fill in the quiet hours of his retirement. And I will look out through that single narrow window that perforates the fortified walls of Spalatum, and, as the blushing sky announces the coming of the day, I will close my eyes, and I will leave this place, and I will find peace at the first hour of dawn, that time of the morning when an emperor is most merciful.

❋ ❋ ❋

Postcards from America

JUST OFF THE GOLFE de Gascogne, where the sea-fog rolls like a devil's veil over the jagged rocks, a causeway stretched to a promontory with steep-rising steps. On the promontory a crucifix loomed stark beneath gray clouds threatening rain. Madeleine climbed the steps, drawing her shawl around her shoulders. Waves crashed against the promontory. A crow had fixed its talons into the crown of thorns, and seemed to lick blood from the Savior's scalp.

Beneath the overlapping, nailed feet of Christ was an iron skull, symbolizing the Hill of Golgotha. The skull had a slot. It was a letterbox. Madeleine lifted the flap. There was a rumble of thunder. The crow took flight. And Madeleine removed the seven postcards inside.

Her friends in America!

The wind whipped through her streaming white hair, she walked back down the steps—down through the mist and spindrift that left her untouched and dry. Water sloshed over the umber stones of the causeway, and Madeleine stepped around the puddles and foam.

The first card, postmarked December 14, 1912, showed a Union Pacific steam engine roaring through the Rockies. The words "Welcome to Colorado" arched across the top.

Dearest Madeleine,

Our train stalled on a ledge west of Denver. The tracks were iced-over and had contracted. The river in the gorge was raging, and snow-clumps fell from the ties. Imagine my horror when they started to jump. Men, women, children, entire families, some singly, some hand-in-hand. There was something almost gorgeous in the enormity of it all. I ran to the door of the coach, and descended to the last step. A woman emerged from the adjacent cabin, seemed to be in a trance, held her child over the gorge. "Don't do it!" I shouted. "Don't you see? There's no danger! We'll soon be off again!" She let the baby drop. I screamed, reached for it; and then I realized that I was not reaching down, but up, up to the people in the train, to the passengers looking down on me. It was not they who had jumped but I. The faces gaped in shock. How embarrassing. My husband always warned me the opium would kill me some day.

Love,
Claire Mathers

The next postcard was an aerial photograph of New York City in the late morning. It was postmarked August 5, 1986.

Madeleine,

Thought you might enjoy this. True story about a beggar I met: "Why do you beg?" the angel asked. The towers of Heaven, glass and porphyry, rose behind him. The angel was dressed like a yuppie. The beggar lifted his

palm and said, "I ask only for want, to be deprived of per-
fection, that, by this lack, I may see anew and reaffirm the
plenitude of God's grace." The angel sneered and said, "I
give you nothing but advice. Your being here is proof of
God's grace. Abandon this charade, it is unseemly for a
denizen of this city." And the angel walked away. The
beggar closed his hand over the angel's advice, clasped it
to his breast, and thanked the Almighty for affirming by
this hollow gift His plenitude, His love, and His grace.

Jonny Duncan

Madeleine smiled. Jonny had grown thoughtful in the afterlife, so different from the boy of 23 who died in World War II.

She moved to the next card, postmarked September 8, 1964. A picture in Kodachrome: Beale Street, Memphis. A black woman in a three-quarters length dress with a fur stole stands to one side of a candy store, laughing at the viewer; on the other side, three black men in pinstripes hold lollipops and grin at her.

Hi Madeleine,

Today I left Mr. Baxter's service for good. It was his
birthday. I gave him a box with a pink bow. Widow
Westfall said, "Ruby, that bow reminds me of a little col-
ored child I saw at the candy store on Beale Street last
week. Had on a frilly white dress and wore a bow just like
that." And then she turned to Mrs. Baxter and said,
"Beautiful child."—"That woulda been my cousin,
ma'am," I said. "Ruby," she said, "did you hear about

that bombing at the colored church on Sunday? You know any of the people that died?" I was gonna say "Yes, ma'am, the child you mentioned," but Mrs. Baxter changed the topic, wanted to talk about something less depressing, but not before I saw her husband's snake-eyes slide over to his son, who grinned. I know Mrs. Baxter and Widow Westfall knew what the men had done—my friends and family on the other side of life told me. "Leonard," Mrs. Baxter said to her husband, "Tell everyone about that crazy aunt of yours that killed herself by jumping off a train in winter."—"I has to go, ma'am," I told her. "Go on home, dear. And thanks again for all you did," and she smiled that slick, movie-star smile. I walked quarter-mile driveway. My Uncle Elmer was parked in his truck. I got in and slammed the door, and the Baxter house blew sky high. "Good Lord," I said. "Like to shook half of Memphis."

xoxoxoxo
Ruby

Ruby had been a powerful medium. Madeleine had learned a lot from her when they met in 1971, several years after this postcard was sent.

Madeleine walked down the path to her cabin. The next postcard showed a painted scene of a covered bandstand in a small town called Meredith, Missouri. It was postmarked June 15, 1944.

Miss Madeleine,

My sister Nancy worships you, and I want to learn your arts some day. As you know, Danny Krueger loved

Nancy, but Nancy's eyes were only for Jonny Duncan, and, truth be told, he's a bruiser. Besides, Danny's only a runt of 16. When Jonny's mom received a telegram saying his plane went down in the Marianas, Nancy refused to believe it, and told Danny that Jonny wasn't dead. You should have seen the memorial service the town organized at the park. There wasn't a dry eye there. But when the band struck up a rendition of "God Bless America," we heard a plane engine and looked up. It was dark out, but we saw the belly of a plane pass overhead, right over the bandstand. It was a fighter plane, just like in the newsreels. Nancy turned to Danny and said, "I told you," and sprinted off in the direction the plane had gone. We ran after her, but her footprints disappeared in the field. If you see her, ask her to come home. We miss her terribly.

Disconsolate,
Cecilia

Madeleine rounded a tree with the *ex-voto* limbs of mannequins nailed to it.

Poor Cecilia. She couldn't possibly know that her sister was still dogging the heels of Jonny Duncan in the beyond, never catching him. Jonny showed her pity from time to time, would wait, just long enough to let her see him. And then he would leave. Nancy searched the places where the dead gather. She wandered the unpaved roads that turn to dreams and sky, but never caught him. And for all the wisdom Jonny had gained in the afterlife, he apparently never outgrew the hot-blooded pride and cruelty of the young maverick lover.

But the real tragedy was what happened to the hapless Danny Krueger.

Lightning flashed overhead. The next card had a picture of the Golden Gate Bridge in San Francisco and was postmarked March 20, 1972.

Hi Madeleine,

Last night was like any other. The teleprompt scrolled the news. The cameras and lights were trained on me. "This is Danny Krueger," I said, and launched into a summary of events in Vietnam. "And now in local news," I said. "A woman was stabbed to death this evening in Golden Gate Park by her husband of five years. Police report that after the murder the husband was discovered dead in a fountain close by, his wrists slashed in an apparent act of suicide. More on this when we return." The boy handed me a file, I opened it. And there was Ruby, my beloved, each wound like a cadaver's lips on her black skin. "Why did you do it?" the cameraman asked. "She found another," I said. "But sixty-three stab wounds?" the cameraman asked. "I had already lost my beloved Nancy. I couldn't lose Ruby too. I can't explain it," I said. And then I felt the blood oozing from my wrists, and the pages of the police report overspread with it. How lonely this life was. How banal and uninteresting its end; a lurid segment, sensational and brief, preceding a commercial break.

Danny Krueger

Madeleine and Ruby had shared a small shop, selling medicines and potions in the early '70s.

"I fired up the stove and worked the roots last night, Madeleine," Ruby said. "There's something wrong with

Danny. I know he's older than me. And I know that men have different changes they go through. But Danny still has eyes for that girl Nancy that left him when he was a boy. And I've seen this Nancy. She's dead, Madeleine, and she don't care for Danny—not in the beyond, and never really cared for him when she was alive. But I'm gonna make Danny snap out of it."

"How?" Madeleine asked.

"A Haight-Ashbury homo friend of mine is gonna pose as my new man. And I'm gonna make Danny love me again." And she smiled, and so had Madeleine, although uneasily.

"You shouldn't do that," Madeleine had said, and felt bad, because her accent had at that time been so thick that it sounded as if she were encouraging Ruby.

Madeleine opened the door to her house. The cats nuzzled her legs. She snapped her fingers at one that was on the kitchen counter inspecting a headless frog. "Get down," she said. And it did.

The next postcard showed a vibrantly painted picture of boys camping in a place called Twin Lakes, Indiana. It was postmarked July 9, 1932.

Dear Madeleine,

I took the boys from my Sunday school class at Meredith Church to the Potawatomi Trail in Indiana last weekend. It rained. We camped in a cave. The boys were exhausted, climbed into their sleeping bags. We built a small fire, but were asleep by midnight. Then we woke, and instantly tensed up. There was chanting in a language we didn't know. I heard the boys whimpering. The oldest, Jonny Duncan, sprang from his sleeping bag and crept over to the shadows in the far corner of the cave. And then, out of nowhere, a man appeared behind us at the cave's mouth and said, "The voice you hear, boy, says that you are like an eagle. You will fly up to the heavens, but your wings will flame and burn you down, like the dying flame in that fire. And that is what the voice says." And the stranger simply walked away, and we could hear his feet squelching in the mud. It was still raining outside. The chanting stopped. I found my flashlight and turned it on. There was no one else in the cave, but when we went to the far end, where we thought we had heard the voice, we found a skeleton in the garb of a medicine man. I can't tell you what a scare it caused us, especially Jonny Duncan.

Your Friend,
Henry Mather

Madeleine leaned back in her chair. The last postcard was a black-and-white from the turn of the century. It was tinted with powder-blues and pinks, showing a woman on the Pont Neuf in Paris, holding a parasol in one hand and a fish in the other. The superscription read "Poisson d'Avril". There was no postmark, but the message at the back was dated April 1, 1899.

My name is Samuel Mather. You do not know me. I am descended from the great witch hunter, Cotton Mather. My son, Henry, is a good Christian, and I have expectations for him. As for my wife, Claire, I fear the dragon she chases will catch her one day. I traveled from Boston. I arrived yesterday in Paris. I saw you pass the church of St. Germain, saw you look at me, and in that instant knew the powers you harbor. I was drawn to you, rose from my seat under the canopy of Les Deux Magots. I followed you, but could not keep pace. I saw you receding from me down the Left Bank. And then you crossed the Pont Neuf, and were lost in the crowd. I wiped my brow with my kerchief. And then I saw this card, which seemed an exact and faithful reproduction of you. It was a "Poisson d'Avril" card. How funny...But it is I who am the fool. I shall write this message to you. I will ask my son to bury this postcard with me in the churchyard at Salem when the great call comes. Maybe one day it will come to you, my Beloved.

Yours faithfully,
Samuel Mather

Madeleine looked at the picture, she remembered the photographer, the man whom she had rewarded with a kiss that killed him before he could sin. "Did I ever look so young?" she said, and then she laid the postcards on the table beside her. The rotary phone rang, she picked up the receiver.

"Halo?" she said. "Oui, c'est Madeleine." And then a pause. And then in accented English, "Funny that you should call. Your postcard arrived today."

The next morning she sat at her booth in the picturesque town on the Golfe de Gascogne. And the tourists passed by. The boxes on the table in front of her were filled with antique postcards, and a German was perusing them. The vendor to her left sold old coins; the one to her right, old stamps.

The German held four postcards in his hand and was studying a fifth. It was a photograph of the Sebilj fountain in Sarajevo, taken in 1993. She remembered it well. Her hair had become iron-grey by then. She had stood over the body of a Bosnian shopkeeper, blood gushing from the bullet hole in his head. She had taken the card from the rack beside him. And then a man in uniform came at her, yelling and waving a pistol. She dropped the card. It fell to the ground. But when the Serb raised his gun to fire, a sniper's bullet struck him in the temple and he fell beside the Bosnian, their blood pooling together, the postcard's edge stained.

"Wouldn't it be funny," the German said in fluent French, "if this were a bloodstain? And if it were from the Bosnian war?" And then he looked at her and smiled. "But you would not have remembered this. Do you run the booth by yourself?"

"Yes," she said.

"How old are you?" he asked, a lascivious glint in his eye.

"Fourteen," the child Madeleine answered, her response blunt, cold.

The German regarded her warily. "How much for these?"

"There are five, so it will be 25 euros, Monsieur."

He paid and left. The sky was overcast. She wondered if creatures like the German knew when they had committed a transgression that had doomed them to swift death. He would make it to Hamburg, but he would die in the Bahnhof from heart-failure, overturning a rack of postcards as he fell.

She closed the booth and padlocked it. And then she sprinted through the streets of the small town. She ran out of it—ran to the causeway, to the promontory with the cross. The sky was thickening. And when she reached the steps, the child Madeleine pulled seven postcards from the pocket of her dress and flung them into the air. They rose, fluttering over the cross, over the sea. The wind bore them up. And then, as gradually as shadows spread at dusk, the postcards tumbled into the clouds, and into the rumble of the coming storm.

ABOUT THE AUTHOR

Daniel W. Davison graduated from Indiana University
in 1997. His hobbies include collecting rare and
unusual books that few have ever read or ever will.
This is his first attempt at making one.

THE RAMSAY PRESS
publishes small editions of books
of scholarly or literary interest.

www.ingramcontent.com/pod-product-compliance
Lightning Source LLC
Chambersburg PA
CBHW051248170626
46809CB00004B/1552